THE 3 INVESTIGATORS

"WE INVESTIGATE ANYTHING"

Jupiter Jones, Founder
Pete Crenshaw, Associate   Bob Andrews, Associate

Jupe is the brain. Pete is the jock. And Bob is Mr. Cool. Together they can solve just about any crime in Rocky Beach, California.

But can they ambush a band of guerrilla fighters who are planning a big-bucks robbery?

This could be all-out war!

THE THREE INVESTIGATORS
C R I M E B U S T E R S

THE 3 INVESTIGATORS

CRIMEBUSTERS™ #8

Shoot the Works

by
WILLIAM McCAY

based on characters created by Robert Arthur

Borzoi Sprinters
ALFRED A. KNOPF • NEW YORK

DR. M. JERRY WEISS, Distinguished Service Professor of Communications at Jersey City State College, is the educational consultant for Borzoi Sprinters. A past chair of the International Reading Association President's Advisory Committee on Intellectual Freedom, he travels frequently to give workshops on the use of trade books in schools.

A BORZOI SPRINTER PUBLISHED BY ALFRED A. KNOPF, INC.
Copyright © 1990 by Random House, Inc.
All rights reserved under International and Pan-American Copyright Conventions. Published in the United States by Alfred A. Knopf, Inc., New York, and simultaneously in Canada by Random House of Canada Limited, Toronto. Distributed by Random House, Inc., New York.

CRIMEBUSTERS is a trademark of Random House, Inc.

Library of Congress Cataloging-in-Publication Data
McCay, William.
Shoot the works / by William McCay ; based on characters created by Robert Arthur.
p.   cm.—(The 3 investigators. Crimebusters ; #8)
Summary: The Three Investigators track down a gang who are using paintball war games as a training ground for crime.
ISBN 0-679-80157-X (pbk.)
[1. Mystery and detective stories]   I. Arthur, Robert.
II. Title.   III. Series.
PZ7.M4784136sh   1990
[Fic]—dc20   89-37749

RL: 6.1
Also available in a library edition from Random House, Inc.—
ISBN 0-679-90157-4

Manufactured in the United States of America
10   9   8   7   6   5   4   3   2   1

1

Fresh Meat

"**W**E'RE GONNA GO OUT THERE AND KILL THEM!" Pete Crenshaw's eyes sparkled with excitement as he spoke. For about the fiftieth time, he hefted his holster. He was still getting used to the weight of a pistol at his hip.

"I wonder if General Custer said that before he was completely surrounded by Indians," Jupiter Jones said. He gave Pete an envious glance. From the old fatigue hat on his reddish-brown hair to the scuffed hiking boots on his feet, Pete looked the perfect soldier of fortune—all six feet one of him in a camouflage-pattern jumpsuit.

Jupe was wearing the same kind of suit—but it made *him* look like a government-issue blimp. His ample stomach strained the camo-pattern fabric, and he needed two web gunbelts to hold up his holster. Even so, it kept sliding below his waistline.

With his black hair sticking out from under a dopey-looking "authentic" boonie hat, Jupe suspected he resembled a prize jerk. He had been looking forward to the end of the spring semester at Rocky Beach High to work on some special projects of his own. None of them involved physical exertion, let alone guerrilla war.

Jupe shone when he was using his mind—working on his computer or solving the mysteries he and his two best friends tackled as The Three Investigators. They had formed the amateur detective team in their early teens and had surprised Rocky Beach, California, with their successes. But Jupe had a strong feeling that his mind wouldn't help him much today.

"How did we get roped into this?" he whispered to Bob Andrews, who with Pete and Jupe completed the detective team.

Bob looked like Hollywood's version of the super soldier. His rented jumpsuit fitted him as if it were tailor-made. The black beret on his blond hair made him look like the perfect seventeen-year-old heart-throb—which most of the girls in Rocky Beach thought he was.

Now he just grinned and shrugged. "Seems to me Pete and Kelly dreamed this up."

"Stop griping, you know you'll go for this," Kelly Madigan said as she came up, cinching her belt tighter around the waist of her jumpsuit. "What do you think?" she asked Pete, twirling around.

"Looks good to me," Pete told her, taking in her trim camo-clad figure. With her suntanned skin and long brunette hair, Kelly looked like a cheerleader going off to war—which was exactly what she was.

"Maybe we should have pictures *before*," Jupe said,

"because I know that we're going to get pulverized. Absolutely *pulverized*."

"Look, you don't get pul—" Kelly shook her head. "Nobody gets hurt playing paintball. It's just like Capture the Flag."

"Except everyone dresses like commandos and packs weapons that would scare Rambo," Jupe said, patting the gun at his hip.

"Hey, hang loose," Bob put in. "It's just an air gun. A whiff of carbon dioxide knocks out a little ball of paint. If it hits you, you get covered with paint—that's it."

Jupe looked unconvinced. "And exactly how fast is this paintball traveling?"

"Just about three hundred feet a second," a voice behind him cut in.

Jupe turned to see a beefy, blond-haired guy who looked like a football player gone to seed. Like everyone else around, he was wearing a camouflage suit— in his case, a bush jacket and fatigue pants. He smirked at Jupe.

Jupe hardly noticed. He was busy calculating.

"Holy Toledo! That's about two hundred miles an hour!" Jupe said. "Even if Jell-O hit you at that speed it would hurt."

"You look pretty well padded to me," said a guy sporting a Marine-style crew cut. "Checkin' out the recruits, are you, Flint?" he said, socking the blond man in the arm. "That's the best part of these open games—the fresh meat." The crew-cut guy's features were as sharp as the crease in his uniform—and his grin looked downright bloodthirsty.

A third man with a heavy black mustache joined them. "Ignore these bozos. They're just trying to psych you out. My name's Vince Zappa. This is Nick Flint," he said, gesturing to the big blond guy, "and this is Art Tillary." He nodded at the crew cut.

Jupe, Pete, Bob, and Kelly introduced themselves. Then the three strangers moved off to join the growing crowd around the target range.

"Let's get over there," Pete said. "I think they're ready to teach us how to use our guns."

A man wearing a Day-Glo orange vest stood in front of the target range. He had a bullhorn in one hand and a paint gun in the other. "Hi, everybody," he bellowed through the bullhorn. "I'm Bob Rodman— call me Splat. Welcome to Battleground Three in the wild Los Angeles hills. Listen up, especially you new-comers. Now—a paintball battle lasts about forty-five minutes."

Jupe breathed a sigh of relief and quietly set his watch alarm. In three quarters of an hour he would be out of this, no matter what.

Splat Rodman was saying, "We have strict rules around here. Don't use a gun unless you're on the field or here in the firing range. When you're in these areas, goggles *must* be worn. If the staff finds you without goggles, you're sidelined for the rest of the day. Now, here's how to load your gun. . . ."

Splat showed them how to slip a CO_2 cartridge into the butt of a gun and how to attach the tube of ten paintballs to it. Then he turned and emptied his pistol at some of the targets on the range. *Pop-pop-pop* went the gun, with a click in between as Rodman worked the bolt action to reload.

I could be spending my Saturday trying out that new program I just bought for my computer or testing out my new car, Jupe thought. What are The Three Investigators doing in the middle of a war zone? We're supposed to be solving mysteries, not playing GI Joe in the woods!

He glanced at his friends. Pete was totally absorbed by the demonstration. Kelly was looking proudly at Pete. And Bob was scanning the crowd of paintballers—no doubt to see if there were any pretty girls around.

Splat was now explaining the rules of the game, but the Investigators had trouble hearing him. Jupe's stomach was growling—loudly.

"What's it this week?" Bob wanted to know.

"Huh?" Jupe said.

"What diet are you on now?" Jupe always seemed to be committed to some bizarre scheme to lose weight.

"Is it chopped Uniroyals?" Pete asked, grinning hugely.

"Or computer chips with guacamole?" Bob added.

"If you *really* want to know," Jupe said stiffly, "it's high fiber. You know, oat bran, broccoli, raisins. They clean you right out."

"Yeah. I can hear the vacuum cleaner running from here," Pete said, stifling a laugh.

Rodman set up the day's first game. "Along with goggles and paintballs, everyone got a red or yellow bandanna on the way in. Tie it around your left arm—that tells the others what team you're on. When you're hit, take the bandanna off and hold it over your head. Once you do that, no one can shoot you." He stared hard at the assembled crowd. "Understood?"

A chorus of yesses came back to him.

"Right. Some of our regular competition teams are here today, but not enough members showed for a full professional tournament. So we'll just be playing an open game. You regulars might remember that and take it easy on the walk-ons." Rodman gave his audience another stern look. "Now, on the Red Team are some guys from Splatforce Three—our home team— all of the Magnificent Seven, and a few newcomers."

The Investigators and Kelly looked at their bandannas. "We're all on the Red Team," Pete said.

"The Yellow Team has regulars from Gorilla Warfare and the Cactus Crawlers, plus the rest of the walk-ons," Rodman finished.

"This'll be like shooting fish in a barrel," Nick Flint said as he tied on a yellow bandanna.

"More like whales," Art Tillary answered. His armband was also yellow.

Team Yellow walked off to its starting place. The Investigators and Kelly put on their goggles and followed the Red Team. They marched through the graveled parking lot and into the sandy, scrubby hills overlooking Los Angeles.

Pete was busy checking out the terrain. "Guys, we can duck for cover behind these bushes or in those woods below us."

A low-pitched gurgle sounded from close by.

"What was *that*?" asked Kelly.

Bob and Pete looked at Jupe.

The leader of The Three Investigators looked embarrassed. "All this exercise is stimulating my appetite. I'm starving! Why don't we duck for cover behind the refreshment table?"

"What happened to high fiber?" Bob said.

"Oh, give it a rest." Jupe stomped off after the Red Team. He could easily tell who the experienced competitors were. They were decked out like enlistment posters for the Marines. Their paint guns had customized stocks, pump-action reloaders, special feeding tubes to hold more paintball ammunition, and extended barrels. One guy even wore a camo-pattern hockey mask with a weird smile painted on it. That plus a black beret and super-customized gun made him look like the Mad Murderer of Beverly Hills.

Vince Zappa and another high-tech Red Team player were studying a map and plotting strategy.

"Suppose the Magnificent Seven guard our flag, with Splatforce ready for a counterattack. The new guys and lone wolves will spread about halfway down the field in a skirmish line."

After some haggling with the other regulars, that plan went through. An air horn sounded, marking the beginning of the game. The Investigators, Kelly, and three other Red Team members set off for the wooded valley that marked the middle of the roped-off playing field.

"Let's spread out," one of the lone wolves said. Another—the guy with the hockey mask—nodded and disappeared into the woods.

The Investigators headed over to the tape stretched at the left edge of the playing area. They chose positions within sight of one another, taking cover behind trees or clumps of brush.

Another gurgle broke the nervous silence.

"Good grief, Jupe," Bob whispered, "tell your stomach to chill out."

Kelly smothered a giggle.

"I can't help it if my digestive juices—*yowch!*" Jupe spun around, displaying a large splat of orange paint on his back.

He felt annoyed but relieved. This game was over for him. Now he could go back to being an ordinary California teenager on summer vacation. He stopped the alarm on his watch, took off his bandanna, and waved it in the air.

"So long, macho men," Jupe said as he turned to go.

"They got Jupe!" Bob began pumping shots into the bushes around Jupe's old position. The blond Investigator's stand was brave, but there was a lot more paint coming at him than from him. In seconds he was hit too.

Then it was Kelly's turn. "Where is everybody?" she whispered. She fired three shots at the underbrush, then her gun seemed to jam. Ducking low behind a tree, she frantically fiddled with the bolt on her pistol, trying to get it to work. Orange paint seemed to explode all around her.

"I need some help here!" she yelled. "Pete Crenshaw, where are you?"

Gun at the ready, Pete ducked from tree to tree, trying to see where the shots were coming from. Although he could hear the *pop-pop-pop* of paintball fire in the distance, the shots aimed at their line were completely silent. He couldn't figure it out.

Beyond him, Kelly was swatting the bushes with her useless pistol, thinking she might surprise a camouflaged Yellow Team member. "You haven't got me yet. Ouch! I take it back." Paint splattered her knee, then her shoulder.

"Okay! Okay! I'm dead, all right? Ow!" Kelly jumped as a third silent shot hit home. "Oh, right, the bandanna. Look! It's off! I'm dead, okay?"

Rubbing her leg, Kelly limped back to the staging area.

Pete had been running to the rescue, only to see Kelly "die." He dove behind a fallen log at the edge of a small clearing, expecting to get zapped himself. He burrowed deep into the leaves mounded against the log. I should be jumping up to make Kelly's attackers pay for that, he thought. But who knows how many guys are out there?

Pete heard footsteps running away, then silence. The Red Team seemed to have abandoned the valley. Pete debated leaving too. The sound of paintball fire came from far off. He wondered again why he hadn't heard the shots that took out Jupe, Bob, and Kelly.

A thin thread of light glinted from under the log. Scrunching down still farther under the leaves, Pete realized he had a long, thin peephole. Through it he saw two pairs of feet heading toward him. He froze.

The feet came within three yards of the log, then stopped. One set of legs wore standard army camouflage—the traditional green-and-brown tree-bark pattern. The other legs had gray-and-brown blotches on sandy brown. There was no way of telling what team the players were on.

"This one is a snap," Gray-and-brown said in a low voice. "We rolled up their picket line. Next stop, their flag." He laughed. "I hope next Friday goes as simply."

"Don't take this too lightly," Tree-bark warned. "Remember—treat the practice run as if it were the real thing. When we have to do this for real, the guards won't be protecting a flag—they'll be watching over a safe with a million in it!"

2

Military Patterns

THOSE GUYS ARE PLANNING A ROBBERY! PETE SAID TO himself. For a split second he considered jumping up then and there to confront the two players.

Good move, a little voice in his head said. Accuse two guys of grand larceny—while you're alone with them in the middle of the woods.

But Pete was dying to know who these guys were. Their voices were too low to identify. He decided on a more cautious plan. He'd stay frozen right where he was until the men had passed by, then he'd take a peek at them.

Pete lay in agony while an assortment of itches, tickles, and urges to sneeze attacked his body. He fought them all off until he was sure it was finally safe to move. Carefully he raised his head over the log—to find that the two guys had disappeared.

Okay, he'd just have to track them down. They'd been heading straight across the clearing, right past the fallen log. That probably meant they'd gone through that empty space between the trees—it looked like a rough trail.

Pete headed down the same way. Before setting foot on the trail, he pulled his paint gun from its holster. The weight of a weapon in his suddenly sweaty palm made him feel a little bit better with potential thieves on the loose.

Five minutes later Pete had to admit that he'd lost his suspects. In fact, he'd even lost the trail. He found himself struggling through heavy underbrush against a rising hillside. Pete thought he was heading in the direction of his team's flag station. He'd come down into the valley on a nice, wide, bulldozed path. That seemed to have disappeared, but it had to be around here somewhere.

The silence in the woods was creepy. Where *was* everyone? Finally Pete heard the familiar *pop-pop-pop* of paintball fire. It came from ahead, off to the left, sounding like a muted version of the Fourth of July. These people were throwing a lot of paint.

Pete set off at a run, angling across the side of the hill. At the top he had a view of his team's flag station. Jupe's words before the game came back to him. The situation *did* look like Custer's Last Stand. Members of the Red Team had taken up defensive positions all around their flag. They huddled behind what cover they could find, taking shots when they could.

Most of the Yellow Team, on the other hand, were laying down a regular barrage of paintballs. That allowed them to dash in closer and closer to the Red flag. There had to be twice as many yellow bandannas down there as red ones. That left practically nobody guarding the Yellow flag at the other end of the field.

A light dawned for Pete. Nobody guarding the Yellow flag? Then I'm gonna go for it!

He'd done crazier things in football games. If he didn't risk everything, the Yellow Team would win.

As he slunk back down the hillside to get into attack position, a real marvel came along. Running up the wide path that led to the flag station came the guy in the beret and green hockey mask.

Draped over his shoulders was a large piece of yellow cloth—the Yellow Team's flag.

Rats! Pete thought. He's beat me to it. But now he has to get the flag to our station.

The flag carrier's problem was to get through the besiegers before they noticed him. Dropping to his belly, the guy began worming his way through the underbrush. He'd gotten halfway to the Red flag station before he was noticed.

"He's got our flag!" one of the Yellow Teamers yelled. "Get him!"

Three guys kneeling behind a stand of trees stood up to take shots. That was Pete's cue. He came charging down the hillside behind them, emptying his gun as he came. With yells of shock, all three "died." Pete reloaded from behind their position and began pumping shots at another clump of Yellow Teamers.

In the confusion of the attack from their rear, Team Yellow wavered. Players jumped for new cover or turned to shoot at Pete. The revived Red Team defenders launched a counterattack.

Ducking a hail of paintballs, Old Greenface brought the flag into the Red Team's station. The referee raised an air horn and let off a blast. Team Red marched back to the gathering area. They'd won!

Pete shook hands and had his back pounded by his teammates, a little amazed at how things had turned out. He was even more surprised when Old Green Face took off the hockey mask and beret to reveal a pretty face and shoulder-length black hair. He was a she!

Standing beside the line of wash basins for cleaning off paint were the other Investigators and Kelly, who had a lot of paint to get rid of.

"Hey, Pete." Kelly waved. "We're over here."

"Here's something to cover your black-and-blue marks," said Pete. He handed them each a patch commemorating the Red Team's victory. Then he herded his friends away from the others.

"Your ears are gonna fall off when you hear this," Pete told them. He repeated what he'd learned in the woods, lying next to the two pairs of feet.

"A safe holding a million dollars?" Bob repeated. "That's not chopped liver!"

"Can we keep food out of this?" Jupe begged. His stomach was crying for cholesterol. "The only real clue is that one of the thieves wore unusual camouflage. And I happen to know where it comes from." He looked smug, waiting for someone to ask.

"Oh, I give up," Pete said. "Where does it come from? And how do you know?"

"While you were playing Davy Crockett, I was talking to Splat Rodman. He, as you can see, is wearing the same pattern." They all turned to look at the operator of the paintball park. Under his Day-Glo referee's vest were the gray-and-brown shapes on a sandy background.

Jupe went on, "They happen to be Rhodesian bush cammies. From the fighting in the African veld in the seventies, before Rhodesia became Zimbabwe. Splat said bush cammies are impossible to see in dry brush—which is just what we have in Southern California in the summer."

"So what do we do with that vital info?" Pete wanted to know. "Move to Rhodesia?"

"You can go if you like, big boy," Kelly said. "I've got cheerleading practice."

"Hey, can it, you guys," Jupiter said. "We're on to something big here. This isn't paintball anymore. It's a case for The Three Investigators!"

"Okay, let's find out who's got those Rhodesian cammies besides Rodman," Bob said.

Observing the players lined up to buy sodas and snacks at the refreshment table, they picked out four men right away: the crew-cut Art Tillary and two other regulars on today's Yellow Team, plus Vince Zappa from their own Red Team.

As the same teams formed for the second game of the day Zappa came up to them, stroking his luxuriant black mustache. "This time we're going to attack. You guys game for a stab into enemy territory?"

"Why not?" Jupiter said. "We've got nothing to lose but our pride."

"Hang in there," Bob told Jupe. "You'll see, we'll get better at this as we go along."

"Let's *do* it," Pete said.

The air horn blasted and the squad of Red Team members set off into the woods. With them was the girl who'd won the last game. She was back in her hockey mask, so Pete looked into a green-plastic face as she shook his hand.

"I'm Lynn Bolt," the girl said. "Thanks for the cover fire. Those guys would have popped me otherwise."

Even as she spoke they crashed into an attacking column from the other team. After a wild, confusing firefight in the woods, neither side got through to the enemy's flag. When the horn blew at the end of forty-five minutes, game two was a draw. But this time Kelly and all the Investigators except Jupe lived through the fight.

"What were you saying about getting better at this?" Jupe demanded of Bob. "That big blond guy, Flint, and his crew-cut buddy, Tillary, *both* got me." He groaned, rubbing his ribs.

"I found out the names of the other two guys on the Yellow Team who're wearing weird cammies," Bob reported. "The tall one with the potbelly is Clayton Pidgeon. He's the captain of Gorilla Warfare. The short, stocky guy with red hair is the second in command. His name is Olson."

"Well, at least we're getting somewhere," Jupe said. "For the next game, let's not go charging off to get shot at. Save our energy for investigating."

Game three saw the Investigators and Kelly guarding the flag while the rest of the Red Team launched a major offensive. But a raiding Yellow Team party burst out of the trees, shot Jupe, and made off with the Red flag to win the game.

"That guy with the crew cut—Tillary—shot me again," Jupe said darkly. "And he *laughed*."

"Don't let it get you down, Jupe," Lynn Bolt said. "You're up against some real pros."

The tally was now one win for each team and one draw. With the last game coming up, both sides were eager to score the tiebreaker. Lynn convinced Pete and the others to go along on another attack, but Jupe asked to be left behind. "I'll stay with the flag," he said.

About halfway across the field the Red Team fell into a Yellow Team ambush. Lynn and Pete managed to survive and retreated toward their own flag station. They picked off a number of Yellow Team players and then Lynn got hit. Pete heard rushing feet coming toward him on the trail from the Red Team's home base. He took cover just in time.

The crew-cut Art Tillary appeared, the Red flag draped over his shoulders.

Splat! Pete covered Tillary with red paint. For a second Pete was stunned. The paint looked almost like blood.

Tillary shrugged and handed the Red flag to Pete.

By the rules, Pete now had to drape the flag over his own shoulders and return as quickly as possible to his home base. He started back along the trail. Behind him, he heard crashing in the underbrush. It sounded as if every Yellow Team member still in the game was coming his way.

Pete put his head down and ran. He made it to the Red Team station and tossed the flag over its rope holder. Drawing his gun, he jumped for cover.

About half of Team Yellow came charging out of the trees. But before they came up the hill, an air horn went off. The game was over. The Red flag was still in position, so the game was a draw, and so was the whole day.

It ended on a note of triumph for Jupe, however. He was liberally spattered with paint, as usual, but grinning widely. "They got me," he said to his friends. "But I got him. Good." He pointed to the blond football type, who was washing off a blotch on his chest.

The blond guy went over to his crew-cut friend in the Rhodesian cammies, then led him toward the Investigators. "I'm Nick Flint, captain of the Cactus Crawlers," he said. "We met earlier. You did great for newbies. Really great."

Art Tillary, the bully with the Marine-style hairdo, stared hard at Jupe. "Well, you got your revenge. You're not fresh meat anymore. Maybe we'll see you around again to get our own back."

"Oh, you can bet on it," Jupe said. Tillary rated as a suspect—one whom Jupe would take special pleasure in nailing.

The newbies sprang for some T-shirts at the supply shop. Pete, Bob, and Kelly got plain camouflage shirts. Jupe picked one with the message I HAD THE TIME OF MY LIFE GETTING KILLED AT BATTLEGROUND III.

As they stood in line they saw the potbellied Clayton Pidgeon come up to Vince Zappa, their friend with the mustache. "I'm surprised you have time to play on Saturdays since you opened your own garage."

"Business is lousy," Zappa said gloomily. "My brother-in-law keeps an eye on the place when I'm not around. He likes it—nobody bothers him."

Pidgeon pointed to a forest-green Mercedes sitting out in the parking lot. "My car's been running a little rough lately. Suppose I drop it off with you tomorrow."

"I'd appreciate the business," Zappa said. "The place is on Ventura Boulevard, near Hayvenhurst."

"Fine. I'll stop by in the morning. Can you get it back to me before I start work on Monday?"

Zappa shrugged. "Sure."

Jupe, shamelessly eavesdropping, turned to his friends. "I think we'll stop by that garage soon," he said. "But tomorrow we've got a score to settle—on Battleground Three!"

3

Target Practice

THE NEXT DAY JUPE PULLED HIS LITTLE FORD ESCORT into the Battleground III parking lot to find it almost as full as the day before. He turned off the motor and proudly patted the steering wheel. It felt great to have a car of his own again. Since his last car had been totaled on a previous case, he'd been stuck driving his uncle's aged pickup. No sex appeal whatever. He wrenched his mind from his vehicle to the case under investigation.

"Could Splat Rodman be the robbery target?" he asked Bob and Pete. "He seems to have a pretty successful operation."

"But pretty expensive to start up," Bob said. "He'd have to buy all those rental guns, lease the use of this land, set up the place." He looked around at the plywood shanties that made up the command center. "I don't think he's got a million dollars stashed away waiting to be ripped off."

"Let's see what we can find out." Pete left the car, slamming his door.

"Hey, watch that," Jupe said protectively, gently closing the other door.

"You'd think this was a Jag," Pete said, grinning broadly.

"Or Jupe's heartthrob," Bob joined in.

Jupe muttered darkly to himself. They walked over to the command post, where Splat Rodman sat at a table, writing on a clipboard. He looked up and smiled. "Oho, the return of the newbies. Sorry, guys, you shouldn't have come so late. I can't fit you onto any teams now."

"Actually, we were hoping to rent some guns and practice shooting," Jupe said. "We'd like to learn a little more about paintball."

"So the bug has bitten," Rodman said, handing them registration forms. "I know how it feels. I got hooked in the early eighties, when the sport was just starting out. We'd run around in the woods with makeshift paint guns and have the time of our lives."

He smiled reminiscently. "I was working in real estate full-time then. I decided to invest in a second business I could enjoy—and that turned into Battleground One."

"So you've got three of these places now?" Bob asked.

Rodman nodded. "I've only just opened this one, but it's already my favorite. Besides the big wild section you fought on yesterday, I've got a couple of other smaller, special fields." He grinned. "We've created forts, trenches, sheds, even a little town."

He collected their forms and got up from behind the table he'd been working at. "Well, I'm sure you're more interested in getting your guns and ammo than in wasting time talking to me." Rodman led the way to a locked shed, went inside, and handed over three gun and equipment sets. "Just give me back the bandannas," he said, "and I'll let you guys do your thing."

"Business looks great," Jupe said.

"Weekends are always busy." Rodman shrugged. "We're also open during the week. As the days get longer, teams often show up after work to practice."

He smiled mysteriously at the Investigators. "Now pump that paint. I may have an interesting proposition for you later."

"So he's got a proposition for us," Jupe said as they stood on the firing line, goggles on and guns loaded. "I wonder if it involves a date with a million dollars."

"He's got all these paintball pros to choose from. Why would he bother with a bunch of rookies off the street?" Pete squeezed off a shot into the chest of a plywood cutout, then pumped the gun to reload.

Next to him Bob fired, catching his target in the arm. "Maybe he's trying to impress us. You know, most of the guys who were playing yesterday seemed like pretty solid citizens. I overheard two of the guys talking about their jobs. One teaches psychology at UCLA and the other is a doctor."

"Well, we'll just have to wait and find out." Jupe picked a target, shot—and missed. "Rats."

They continued to practice, using up the ammunition that came with the guns. Soon after Jupe returned from buying a fresh supply, Splat Rodman appeared at the entrance to the firing line.

"How'd you guys like some revenge?" he asked, grinning. Standing beside him was Nick Flint, the blond guy built like a quarterback. "The captain of the Cactus Crawlers here has brought over three of his guys to practice, and he'd like to do it against some live opposition. Whaddaya say?"

Bob looked down at his chinos and polo shirt. "We'd have to rent some of those camouflage jumpsuits."

"And I don't like the odds—four to three," Jupe said.

"You'll be playing defense in one of the special fields—there'll be lots of cover," Rodman said.

"And to sweeten the deal, you'll have three of *these* as equalizers," Flint said, holding up the gun he was carrying. The matte-black weapon looked more like a rifle. It was much bigger than the pistols in the Investigators' hands.

Pete noticed that there wasn't a bolt or a reloading pump under the barrel. "Is that what I think it is?" he asked. "A paintball machine gun?"

Rodman nodded. "I've been debating allowing people to use them on the field—maybe even renting some of them out. So I got a few to test."

"They look pretty good to me," Flint said, stepping up to the firing line. He moved the gun in a wide arc, squeezing the trigger. With the sound of a corn popper going crazy, the gun sprayed paint across four of the man-size cutouts.

The blond-haired Flint looked at the Investigators, a challenging gleam in his eyes. "What do you say, guys?"

"I don't know," Jupe said, not wanting to get sidetracked from the investigation. Why waste time playing games when they could be preventing a million-dollar heist?

Pete just looked at the gun and smiled. "We each get one of these? Let's do it!"

After the guys got into their gear, Rodman led them down another bulldozed path, away from yesterday's playing field. They also met the other three members of Flint's team. Tillary—the mean guy with the crew cut—they already knew. The other two were Herb Gatling, a shovel-jawed guy with dark frizzy hair escaping from under his fatigue cap, and Frank Hare, a slightly pudgy man with a perpetual frown and a boonie hat pulled low over his eyes. All the Cactus Crawlers wore standard Army uniforms—except Tillary. He was in Rhodesian cammies.

Rodman turned off the path at a sign that said HAMBURGER HILL. They followed a smaller trail to the crest of a wooded hill overlooking a clearing with several crude plywood sheds. Beyond them, at the summit of a smaller rise, a set of trenches had been dug, built up with sandbag walls to create a fort.

"Here's the deal," Flint said. "You guys start in

those sheds, we start back here on this hill. Your job is to keep us from getting into the fort. We keep playing until one side or the other is eliminated."

Two of the sheds faced the hillside where the Cactus Crawlers were. The third was a little farther back and set at an angle. Each shed had a front and back entrance with waist-high doors that left the upper doorway open for firing through. Jupe and Bob took the front positions, leaving Pete in the angled shed.

Pete checked his supply of paintballs. He peered out the front doorway, trying to see what was going on at the top of the hill.

All he saw was Splat Rodman. "Ready?" the battleground owner called down to them.

"Ready!" Jupe responded.

"Then—GO!" Rodman disappeared back into the trees. A moment later Art Tillary burst out of the wood line and dashed across an open space to a clump of bushes. The Investigators' machine guns chugged a rain of paintballs at him. He hit the dirt, his hat flying off to reveal his crew cut.

Squirming desperately on his belly, Tillary managed to reach a scrawny bush. He cowered behind it, pinned down.

Nick Flint, Gatling, and Hare took turns popping out from behind trees and splatting shots onto the guys' sheds. They were quickly driven back to cover by the machine-gun barrage.

"Art!" Pete heard Flint yell. "Go for it now!"

All three of Tillary's teammates appeared then, sending quick fire at the two front sheds. Figuring that the Cactus Crawlers were trying to cover Tillary's retreat, Pete leaned out his doorway in the rear shed and splashed a few paintballs around the scrawny bush. This was starting to be fun!

But when a return shot splatted onto his door, he ducked back to safety.

After their covering attempt failed, the Cactus Crawlers went back to single sniping. That went on for a few minutes, with neither side hitting anybody. Pete anxiously scanned the hillside. Sooner or later a member of the other team would show. And then . . .

Pop! Splat! A paint gun fired outside the door behind him, and a paintball smacked into his back.

Pete whirled around. His mouth dropped open when he saw frizzy-haired Gatling and pudgy Hare standing in the doorway, fingers to their lips. He shrugged and nodded. They'd gotten him fair and square. While he and his friends had been protecting against a frontal attack, Flint had sent half his guys on an end run. And it had paid off. Pete watched in silence as the two crept up to the rear doors of the other sheds. Two more shots, a pair of pained yelps, and the game was over.

Jupe and Bob stepped out, sourly rubbing their backs. Tillary came down the hill, grinning. "Guess we pounded your tails this time," he said.

Flint, the captain, was more critical. "Art, you were too slow. If you'd made it to decent cover, you could have been firing, too, instead of leaving me alone to snipe while the flanking force was away."

He turned to Hare and Gatling. "And you two certainly took your time. What was the idea of ganging up on Crenshaw? While one took him out, the other should already have been moving on Jones. Then you could have hit Andrews from either side."

"Pretty slick," Bob muttered to his pals.

"Yeah?" Jupe said. "Why are they getting so uptight about a Sunday-afternoon game?"

"You were good enough to take us all out, anyway," Pete said to the Cactus Crawlers. "That was real commando-style—were all you guys soldiers?"

Flint gave a bark of laughter. "Soldiers? I only wish. Tillary is an accountant in real life. Gatling's an insurance man, and Hare sells cars. I think Gatling was a Boy Scout—does that count?" The other three Cactus Crawlers looked embarrassed.

Flint studied the Investigators for a moment. "Thanks for the game—maybe we'll do it again, huh?" Then he returned to his military critique of the Cactus Crawlers' performance. Pete and his friends had definitely been dismissed.

Jupe, however, watched Flint with suddenly narrowed eyes. "You know," he said quietly to his friends, "if I were going to plan a robbery, that's just the kind of guy I'd want. I wonder what he does when he's not playing commander in chief."

Flint looked at his watch. "Okay, guys, that's it. I've got a late shift today. Let's keep practicing our hand signals, and I'll see you all here Wednesday evening."

The Cactus Crawlers took off, with the defeated Investigators trailing behind. Pete, Bob, and Jupe turned over their machine guns and other gear to Rodman, and reached the parking lot just as Flint was starting his car.

"Get in, guys—hurry," Jupe said, unlocking his car. "And easy on the doors." Pete and Bob exchanged glances.

Flint drove out of the lot, and Jupe followed. Jupe kept well behind him all the way to Santa Monica Boulevard. Then, in the heavier traffic, he pulled a little closer to the man's battered Camaro.

"Jupe, what are you doing?" Bob asked.

"Tailing Flint," Jupe answered. "In case he was the guy in regular cammies that Pete overheard yesterday. He said he had a late shift, so he must be going to work. That gives us a chance to see what he does. No big deal."

Flint stayed on the boulevard until he made a sudden right onto Beverly Drive. Jupe hurriedly swung after him. Flint led them through a complicated course on the various drives and ways of Beverly Hills. Finally he pulled into a parking lot.

Jupe pulled in, too, intending to roll on past the building at the far end and see what it was. Instead he found himself being sandwiched between two police cars. Two more boxed him in front and back. Eight annoyed police officers glared down at the Three Investigators as Flint came over.

Pete read the sign on the rear of the building. BEV-
ERLY HILLS P.D.

"Oh, great," Bob said. "He's a Beverly Hills cop."

"That's right," Flint said, leaning in Jupe's window.
"And I want an answer. What are you doing tailing
me?"

4

Tuning Down

JUPE WAS OVER THE SHOCK—NOW HE WAS WORKING ON embarrassment. He was also trying to come up with some kind of answer to Nick Flint's question as the blond, muscular guy loomed over Jupe's little car.

"Uh, well," he began, looking up into the officer's stony eyes. "I was losing a bet."

"What?" Flint said.

"After watching your team in action, I bet Bob here that you were actually a military man. He said you weren't." Jupe dug into his pocket and pulled out a couple of crumpled bills. "Looks like you win, Bob."

Flint looked amused. "You came close, Jones. Up till two years ago I was in the Army—military police."

"And acts as if he's still in it," one of the other officers muttered.

Flint darted a glance at the mutterer but spoke only to Jupe. "Okay, I guess it's nothing important. But I think you've learned a lesson about pulling stupid stunts. Now clear out of here."

The Investigators were never happier to hear those words.

As they headed back home to Rocky Beach, Bob said, "What do you think, Pete? Should I hold on to this money, having won it?"

"I don't know," Pete replied, teasing. "That wacky show *Truth Is Stranger Than Fiction* might want to put it on TV. I can see it now . . . 'The only money Jupiter Jones ever let go of without a machine gun pointed at his head.' Or maybe we should each keep a dollar as a souvenir—proof that for once in his life Jupe was wrong."

"I just wanted to see what the guy did for a living," Jupe said from behind the wheel.

"Well, we certainly found out—in the most embarrassing way," Bob said. "He's a cop. I think that lets him off our suspect list, don't you?"

"The other cops don't like him," Jupe pointed out.

"So he won't get the precinct's Mr. Congeniality prize," Bob said. "I just don't think he's a suspect."

"Well, who is?" Pete asked.

"Let's go over what we've got so far," Jupe began. "Pete overheard two expert paintballers talking about a million-dollar robbery. One wore standard army camouflage. The other wore Rhodesian bush camouflage. The guys we've seen wearing Rhodesian cammies are Arthur Tillary, Mr. Personality. Splat Rodman, the guy who runs Battleground Three. Clayton Pidgeon—"

"The tall guy with the potbelly," Pete said.

"And Olson, the red-haired stocky guy," Bob said.

"Right," Jupe told them. "And last but not least, Vince Zappa. The guy with the black mustache who owns a garage."

"That makes five," Pete said.

"Tillary's with the Cactus Crawlers," Jupe added. "Pidgeon and Olson are on Gorilla Warfare. Zappa is one of the Magnificent Seven."

"Give me a break!" Pete protested. "I can't remember all that!"

"Never mind. I'll keep track," said Jupe.

"Okay, what do we do now?" asked Bob.

"Let's head back to Headquarters," Jupe said. "I want to talk to my cousin about Vince Zappa. I figure Ty's probably heard about him on the mechanics' grapevine."

"Why Zappa?" Pete wanted to know. "He was the *nice* one. And he was on our side."

"Zappa was also away from the flag station, scouting, while you were hiding under your log," Jupe said to Pete. "I found that out while I was buying ammunition today—before we wound up playing games. Maybe he was meeting someone. And what better place for a secret meeting than the middle of the woods?"

Pete shrugged. "Okay, he's a maybe. Let's see what Ty's got to say about him."

They drove into the junkyard owned by Jupe's aunt and uncle. The yard was the Jones family business, and it was a lot more than the average junkyard. It stocked every weird item Jupe's Uncle Titus could get his hands on—from player-piano rolls to left-handed toast forks. Jupe's cousin, Ty Cassey, hung out there between jobs at local garages.

The Investigators passed their trailer headquarters and stopped at the grease pit Pete had set up next to it. Ty Cassey had just finished working on his car for the zillionth time.

"Hey, guys," he said, wiping oil off his hands with a rag. "What's happening?"

"We were out playing paintball yesterday, and we met a guy you might know," Jupe said to his cousin. "His name's Vince Zappa. He's got his own garage."

Ty nodded. "Yeah, I know Vince. He's a really good mechanic. And yeah, I heard he's really into macho paintball. On a team, or something. But what's he doin' paintballing on a Saturday? That's prime time at garages."

Jupe shrugged. "From what I overheard, it didn't sound as if his garage is busy at all,"

"Yeah, I did hear something like that," Ty said. "Vince is one of the best mechanics in town. But settin' up in business for yourself, that takes money. You need a garage and lots of expensive gizmos to test all the high-tech stuff they put in cars these days. Either you gotta have low overhead or some high-powered car company behind you. And Vince hasn't got either. The guy might just go broke one of these days."

"Would he be desperate enough to steal if he needed money?" Jupe asked. It sounded as if Vince Zappa had a powerful motive.

"Vince? Steal?" Ty laughed. "He's as honest as I

am. Hold on, let me rephrase that," he said, seeing the dubious looks on the Investigators' faces. "Vince would haul in a lot more dough if he dreamed up more problems on the cars that come in—like other guys do. He won't—and that's why he's goin' broke."

"I'd like to check Zappa out," Jupe said to Ty. "Can you do some work on my Escort?"

"Whaddaya mean?" Ty looked a little surprised. "I just tuned it up this week."

"I know," Jupe said. "I'd like you to tune it *down*— give it lots of problems. Then we'll see what Zappa does."

A slow smile replaced Ty's look of puzzlement. "Mess it up, huh? Well, I guess I can louse up the timing and disalign those wheels I worked so hard to align just right."

His smile broadened. "Pete, do me a favor and look in the garbage bin over there. I just pitched six of the world's worst spark plugs from this car—they've got Jupe's name on 'em. And I bet we can find a rotten battery around here somewhere. The big question is, how can we get gunk into the exhaust manifold?"

Ty opened the hood. "First, the timing." He went to the crankshaft drive pulley at the front of the engine, where the degree markings for the ignition timing were. A quick yank at the pointer there upset the careful calibration job he'd done.

"Okay, the spark timing is all wrong—that should give you a nice engine knock. Now for those lousy spark plugs." He replaced Jupe's perfectly good plugs with the corroded ones he'd just thrown out.

Ty snapped his fingers. "Oh, here's a cute one." He went to the ignition coil and removed the wire that went from its negative pole to the distributor, switching it with the wires from the starter. "I've just reversed polarity on the coil—that will give the spark plugs even more trouble and cut the engine's power by about half."

Then, after opening the exhaust manifold and shoveling in a few spoonfuls of carbonized oil, followed by a wheel disalignment, Ty officially pronounced Jupe's car ready to crawl off to visit Vince Zappa.

Fighting a front wheel that wanted to take him off the road, Jupe coaxed his car along Ventura Boulevard, looking for Vince Zappa's garage.

"I don't believe that engine," Pete said as he listened to the chugging that came from under the black Escort's hood. "How could you let Ty muck up your car?"

"More to the point," Bob said, "how do you have the nerve to drive this sucker when it sounds like that?" Every hundred yards or so, the exhaust gave vent to a thunderous backfire. Ka-*Pow!* Jupe tried to ignore the unbelieving stares they were getting from passersby. Bob ducked his head low, hoping no one would see him aboard such an obvious clunker.

"Here's Hayvenhurst coming up," Pete said. "The place should be around here somewhere."

Jupe spotted the sign:—V. ZAPPA, AUTO REPAIRS—and took the car through a wobbly turn into the garage's driveway. Belching a cloud of blue smoke, the Escort groaned, shuddered, and finally came to a stop.

Zappa looked much skinnier and less impressive in mechanic's coveralls than in his Rhodesian cammies. But he had the same grin under his big black mustache. "Sounds like you could use some—" His eyes went wide as he recognized Jupe. "Hey, I know you guys."

"We heard yesterday that you had a shop," Jupe said. "And—well, I need some help with old Betsy here. I bought her secondhand, and everything seems to have gone on her at once. My friend tried to help me out"—Jupe pointed to Pete, who blushed and turned away—"but she seems to be running even more ragged."

"I'll see what I can do," Zappa said. "Let's take a look at her."

"I don't want to take you from your other work," Jupe said.

"What other work?" Zappa looked around the nearly deserted garage complex. Only one other car was there—Clayton Pidgeon's forest-green Mercedes. "That job over there is basically charity—tightening a few nuts and bolts. No, I have lots of time to look at your car—and believe me, there's nobody in line ahead of you."

He opened the hood, took a look at the engine, and tsked. "I don't believe anyone could let simple maintenance go so long and still have a running car," he said. "You'd almost have to foul things up on purpose to get it running this bad."

Bob looked at Pete and grinned.

Zappa set to work cleaning fouled equipment, tightening loose connections, testing for bad parts. The more he did, the more he shook his head and muttered.

Jupe let the mechanic get good and engrossed before he started backing away toward the rear of the garage.

He took a quick peek inside the garage office. The desk was covered with unpaid bills, several of them marked PAST DUE.

The shop itself had several empty spots where equipment had obviously once stood. Jupe figured the stuff had been sold or repossessed.

At the very rear of the building Jupe found a metal door. He tried the knob, but it didn't turn. Nor did the door give when he pushed. Locked. Maybe his plastic school ID card could . . .

Jupe saw a shadow on the door and turned to find Vince Zappa standing over him, a frown on his face and a large wrench in his hand.

"What are you doing back here?" the mechanic demanded.

5

Bolt from the Blue

JUPE PASTED A MORTIFIED LOOK ON HIS FACE AS ZAPPA'S free hand grabbed his shoulder. "I thought this was, you know"—Jupe brought his voice down—"the men's room."

The mustached mechanic stared for a moment, then shook his head. "Well, it's not the men's room," he said. "It's a private workshop. The men's room is outside. Come on, I'll get you the key."

He led the way back to his office, took a key off a hook, then marched Jupe outside. "It's over there, on the left," Zappa said, jerking his thumb.

Jupe went into the dingy rest room, let the water run in the not-too-clean sink, and wet his hands. After a couple of minutes he came back out, shaking off the excess moisture. "You know, there aren't any towels in there," he complained.

Zappa slammed down the Escort's hood. "Get in and start it up."

Jupe got behind the wheel, turned the ignition key,

and gave it a little gas. He was amazed to hear his engine purr. "Hey, that's *great!*" he said.

"You still have some work to be done," Zappa told Jupe. "Those wheels need to be aligned, your exhaust system should be cleaned out—and you should fire whoever has been taking care of your car."

Jupe nodded, hiding a grin.

"But I'd need to keep your car overnight for that, and how would you get home? So I'll just give you this bill for the parts and the time I spent . . ."

He quickly scribbled some figures on a sheet of paper and handed it over to Jupe, who read it and gulped.

"Actually, that's what I call my special paintball discount," Zappa said almost apologetically.

Jupe nodded, then dug deep into his pockets.

As the Investigators drove off Bob said, "Hey, the engine sounds even smoother than when Ty tuned it up."

"I guess you get what you pay for," Pete said, smiling.

Jupe gave them a sour look. "It's too bad Sax Sendler doesn't handle comedy acts—I'm sure you guys would make him a fortune." Sax was Bob's boss, a talent agent who booked rock bands in the area. "That bill you two find so amusing just about wiped me out financially. And the only clue we got out of it is a locked door."

"Well, we know that Zappa is a good mechanic," Bob pointed out.

"But do we know he's a good guy?" Jupe asked. "His business is a disaster. So what's so important in that room that he needs to lock it up?"

Nobody had an answer.

"Let's get our heads off the case for a little while," Bob suggested. "We could go to the mall—I'll even pay the freight for a snack." He glanced at Jupe. "I hear the House o' Cookies is making special oat-bran muffins."

Jupe checked his watch. Four thirty. No wonder his stomach was rumbling.

"You're on," Jupe said.

No sooner did they enter the mall's Floor of Food than they heard a commotion behind them.

"My wallet!" a woman yelled. "He's got my wallet!"

A creepy-looking kid ran past them, a woman's wallet in his hand.

"Stop him!" the woman yelled. Pete and Bob took off in pursuit, but the guy had a lead on them. It looked as if he'd make a clean getaway until he passed the House o' Cookies—and a metal tray flew out of the doorway and into his face.

Pete risked a diving tackle at the faltering thief's ankles. Bob joined him, a second later, to land on the guy's shoulders. The woman and a security guard came rushing up, followed by a puffing Jupe.

"That's the one—he grabbed my wallet!" the woman said. And when the guard turned the creep over, he was still clutching the wallet to his chest.

Pete vaguely recognized the security man as an

off-duty cop from the Rocky Beach force. The guard recognized them, too, it seemed. "So," he said with a grin, "the Three Investigators foil another crime."

"We just sat on him," Pete said. "The person who really gets the credit is the one who threw that tray . . ."

He looked at the entrance of House o'Cookies and saw Lynn Bolt standing there, another tray ready in her hands. She was dressed in jeans and a sweatshirt instead of camouflage and a mask, but she was unmistakable. He'd recognize that long black hair and uptilted nose anywhere.

Right now, though, her eyes were much wider than usual. "You guys are The Three Investigators? Hey, I've heard about you—you're some kind of private eyes." She looked at Pete with even greater interest. "That explains how well you reacted on the field yesterday. I guess you've been in lots of tough spots."

"He certainly has," Jupe butted in. "I bet you two could trade some amazing stories." Pete's eyebrows went up. Lowering his voice, Jupe whispered in Pete's ear, "It's a chance to find out about Rodman, at least. Talk to her."

Lynn looked at Pete, smiling brightly. Pete grinned too—hey, she'd noticed him instead of Bob.

"Why don't you two talk for a while?" Jupe said. "Bob and I have to go to the Hardware Center for some—er, plumbing supplies."

As his friends walked off Pete could hear Bob saying, "Plumbing supplies?"

"Most boring thing I could think of," Jupe replied.

Lynn took Pete's arm and they headed toward an empty table. "Looks like your friends have something else they've got to do. What do you say we swap war stories while you wait for them?"

"War stories?" Pete said.

"I'll tell you some of the hairy things that have happened in games I've played—and you can tell me about your cases," Lynn said. "Are you working on one now?"

"Now?" Pete shook his head. "Not really." He did tell her about a recent case they'd cracked at a film studio, one that had wound up in the newspapers. Lynn told him about a big game she'd played in—over a thousand people on each side.

Pete nodded, wondering how to bring up the subject of Splat Rodman. "You know," he said, grabbing an opportunity, "we were back at Battleground Three today, trying some target practice."

Lynn looked surprised. "So you're thinking of coming back for a second helping? I thought maybe you and your blond friend might try it again, but that girl who was with you and the heavy guy—Jupe?—no way."

"Oh, Kelly enjoyed herself, and so did Jupe. We got a chance to talk to Mr. Rodman, and played on one of his special fields. He's certainly putting a lot of money into Battleground Three."

"He's making enough from his other two fields in the mountains," Lynn said. "And from what I hear, his real estate business isn't hurting." She laughed. "Even his home team, Splatforce, has been making a profit lately. They've been practicing a lot, and Splat asked me if I wanted to be a stand-in for a tournament next weekend—with a hefty purse."

"How hefty?" Pete asked.

"Forty thousand dollars."

That was a fairly big figure, all right. But it definitely wasn't the cool million that the two guys in the woods had been discussing.

"Hey." Lynn leaned across the table and grabbed Pete's arm. "If you're really thinking about practicing up for another game, you don't have to do it at Battleground Three. Let me show you another place."

"Sure," Pete said, getting to his feet. "Where?"

Lynn's smile got wider. "My house."

Pete's mind raced. Is Lynn coming on to me? he wondered. Hmmm. But what about Kelly? Lynn *is* kind of cute, though. And a terrific paintballer. Looks my age. Hey, what am I thinking?

He remembered Jupe urging him to find out about Rodman.

"Let's go!" Pete said to Lynn.

On the way out, he waved good-bye to Bob and Jupe at the Hardware Center. Bob gave him a thumbs-up sign when Lynn wasn't looking.

A little while later, Lynn and Pete were heading down the basement steps at Lynn's house. Upstairs was a typical middle-class Southern California home. Downstairs Pete found a weekend warrior's command post.

Half the basement had been given over to a shooting gallery that stretched the length of the house. The far wall behind the cutouts and targets was spattered with paint.

Lynn led the way to the other part of the basement first. Pete saw Lynn's camouflage fatigues, already cleaned, hanging neatly beside her green mask. Two trophies sat on a shelf, along with books and videotapes about paintball. The wall behind was covered with victory patches from paintball fields all around Los Angeles.

What really caught Pete's eye, however, was the large table with the paintball arsenal spread out on it. Three paint guns sat gleaming on the table, obviously just cleaned and oiled. A fourth lay disassembled.

"Wow," Pete said, "you must really take this game seriously to have so many backup weapons."

Lynn laughed. "Actually, I bought only one—the gun I used yesterday. The others are prizes from various tournaments. I was pretty lucky."

"You mean pretty good."

She shrugged. "Anyway, I use them for target practice and sometimes for tournament play." Stepping over to the table, she picked up a long-barreled pistol and came over to Pete. "This gun is very accurate, but on the heavy side." She slipped the pistol grip into his hand, and he hefted it.

"This is a pretty solid gun," he said.

"Want to try it out?" Lynn offered. She took the gun back from Pete, opened the butt, and slipped in a carbon dioxide cartridge. Then she handed him a tube of paintballs, slipped another tube into his varsity jacket pocket, and put goggles on herself and him. "You can load while I set up the gallery."

She went to the paint-spattered wall and flipped a couple of switches. Six plate targets started jerking back and forth, propelled by some sort of moving belt. In addition, two life-size cutouts flipped up and down. One boasted a poster of Rambo. The other was Indiana Jones. If that wasn't enough, a tiny air compressor chugged away, releasing little gusts that let Lynn hang six Ping-Pong balls in midair.

"You expect me to hit those balls from all the way over here?" Pete had the gun ready, but was frowning unhappily at the tiny Ping-Pong balls dancing on their fountains of air.

"We'll work up to it." Lynn loaded a gun for herself. "I'll start off," she said, going into a slight crouch.

The Rambo cutout came up, and she hit it dead on. Then her gun popped rhythmically as she nailed the jerking plates one by one. Finally she went for the really difficult targets—and knocked three Ping-Pong balls off their jets of air.

Lynn turned to Pete, grinning. "Your turn."

Pete was so involved with the shooting, he had totally forgotten the investigation. The cutouts came up, and he hit both targets. The moving plates confused him a little—he missed one when it suddenly jerked back the way it had come.

With three shots left he prepared for the toughest part of the challenge. He raised his gun, lining up the sights at the top . . . and Lynn stepped up behind him, one hand steadying his aiming arm. She was a tall girl, and her lips were just below his ear as she spoke. "The trick here is to keep both eyes open, so you get the deep focus. Take a deep breath, aim, squeeze the trigger, then let the air out."

Pete felt funny having her so close to him, but he followed her instructions and fired. His shot hit the floating ball dead on.

"You're good—very good," Lynn said. "Just the kind of person I'd want on my team."

"Your team?" Pete asked, lining up the next target.

"The Ladykillers," Lynn said. "I've been trying to pull it together for about a month now—and I've got six girls who are interested. We were originally going to try it as an all-girl team, but"—she leaned a little closer to his back—"I wouldn't mind taking on a few good men."

Pete's arm jerked, and his shot went into the ceiling. Lynn pulled away, and Pete turned to face her. "I—uh—hey, I don't know," he said, flustered. "The guys were sort of thinking of trying to join an established team, like Gorilla Warfare. At least, we were going to talk to Clayton Pidgeon . . ."

Lynn looked so annoyed that Pete was glad her gun was empty. "Sure, you go talk to Pidgeon," she said.

"Maybe he'll give you a home loan and a free toaster oven, too."

Pete blinked. "How's that?"

"I guess you don't know Pidgeon all that well," Lynn told him. "He's a vice-president at Coastal Marine Bank!"

6

Squeeze Play

"**P**IDGEON WORKS FOR A *BANK?*" PETE EXCLAIMED. "Maybe that's the tie-in!"

Too late, he bit his tongue. Lynn had made him so nervous he'd said more than he should.

"What tie-in?" Lynn repeated. Then her face lit up. "You *are* on a case, aren't you? And it has something to do with Clayton Pidgeon! Come on, tell me, tell me!"

Looking at Lynn's eager face, Pete decided he'd have to say *something*. He filled her in briefly. "But don't tell anyone, okay? We'll blow the case if word gets out."

"You can depend on me," Lynn said. "And if you need any help, you know who to call." She grabbed a piece of paper and scribbled on it. "Here's my number." She handed it to him.

"Thanks." Pete headed up the stairs.

"And Pete?"

Pete stopped halfway up to see Lynn smiling at him. "At least consider the other thing," she said.

"Ah, yeah, sure," he mumbled, and fled.

After he got home, Pete called Jupe. Jupe fell silent when he heard the news about Pidgeon. Pete could picture his friend pinching his lip—a sign that Jupiter was deep in thought.

"We'll have to meet and set our strategy for getting more information," Jupe's voice finally came over the line. "Why don't we get together this evening and—"

"Not tonight, Jupe," Pete said. "Kelly and I are going to double with Bob and his date. Remember? We asked you, too, but you turned us down." Pete kept himself from saying, *You're too scared of girls to ask one out.*

"Ah—right," Jupe said. "Well, why don't you stop off before you go? I'll do my best to keep it short, and we should be ready to hit the ground running tomorrow morning."

In the end Pete, Kelly, Bob, and his date all wound up at Jupe's for the meeting.

Ellie Dalles, the pretty red-haired girl with Bob, looked a little nervous as they found places to sit around Jupe's indoor workshop at the junkyard. She glanced dubiously at the shelves loaded with electronics equipment—a camcorder, two-way radios, cassette recorders, computer monitors, plus all kinds of circuits and innards squashed into every corner.

"I've never been to a detectives' meeting before," Ellie said.

"Usually it's pretty boring," Bob told her. "At least this one will be short. Right, Jupe?"

"Short, yes," Jupe said, looking over some papers. "Well, I see two jobs ahead of us—getting more information about Clayton Pidgeon and then asking him some questions. Getting Pidgeon's job out of Lynn Bolt was good detective work, Pete. Obviously she's interested in you. So we'll continue to let you handle her—"

"Did you say 'handle'?" Storm clouds began gathering on Kelly's face. "And what exactly do you mean by 'interested,' Jupe?"

Jupe glanced up, a little surprised. "Only that Lynn wants Pete to join a team she's setting up. At least that's what she told him when he was over at her house."

Kelly's head snapped over to Pete. "You were at her house? How come you didn't mention this to me?"

"It's just part of the case," Pete tried to tell her. "Just investigating—"

"Well, maybe I don't want you investigating that pistol-packing Amazon." Kelly stormed to her feet. "And you can spend tonight thinking about that— *alone!*"

Kelly stomped out of the workshop, and Ellie got to her feet. "Look, Bob, maybe this is a bad time for a date. And I have to get up early tomorrow for my summer job. So give me a call sometime and we'll try it again." Then she went after Kelly.

Jupe was still looking at his notes, unaware of the murderous looks the other two Investigators were giving him.

"You know, I spent two whole weeks trying to get this date with Ellie," Bob said.

"Is lover boy losing his touch?" Pete put in.

"It's a shame it turned out this way," Jupe said, still not catching on. "Sometimes I just can't understand Kelly's attitude." Then he smiled. "But if you guys have nothing to do this evening, maybe we can get a jump on our friend Pidgeon."

"It's either that or strangle you," muttered Bob.

Pete's mind had wandered. It had been fun getting to know Lynn. Why did Kelly have to make such a big deal out of it?

Jupe, still oblivious, barreled on. "You have to admit a bank makes a good target for a million-dollar robbery. Is it just a coincidence that a bank VP plays at the same paintball field as some robbers in training? Or is there some deeper connection? How about we check out Pidgeon first thing tomorrow?"

Pete and Bob grudgingly agreed. Bob said he had time off from his job till Thursday, when Sax would be back from vacation.

"Bob, is your father home tonight?" asked Jupe. "Perhaps he could help get us some information." Bob's father was a newspaper reporter.

"Sure, Dad's home," Bob said. "But a quiet evening at home was not in my game plan."

Unaware of Bob's sarcasm, Jupe got into Pete's Firebird and they drove off in grouchy silence.

"Clayton Pidgeon?" Mr. Andrews frowned, trying to recall something. "We got a press release from

Coastal Marine about him just recently—he'd been promoted, I think. Hold on, let me call a couple of people."

A few minutes later he got off the phone with a little more information. "He's a rising star at the bank, their youngest vice-president. My financial friends tell me he's brought in a lot of new business."

"That doesn't sound like a man who'd rob the place," Bob said.

"We'll find out tomorrow morning," Jupe said. "Now, what will we do tonight?"

They played Scrabble. Jupe won.

♦   ♦   ♦

Coastal Marine Bank's headquarters were located in Van Nuys, and the Investigators set off for it in Pete's car as soon as the morning traffic jam was over. Clayton Pidgeon's office was on the main banking floor, so they had no trouble finding his secretary.

"We'd like to speak to Mr. Pidgeon, please," Jupe said, acting his most official.

The woman looked the three teenagers over and said, "May I ask what it's in reference to?"

Jupe was prepared. "It's a private matter. We heard something of interest to him at a sporting event he attended this weekend."

The secretary shrugged, her finger going to the intercom button on her phone.

Before she hit it, however, the door behind her opened and Clayton Pidgeon stepped out. "I'm going to talk to F.J. about the Encino deal," he said. As he looked at the Investigators he halted for a second.

Then recognition crossed his face, and he was past them—fast. "It will be a long meeting, Marge," Pidgeon said over his shoulder as he rapidly disappeared. "Don't know when I'll be back."

"Uh, Mr. Pidgeon . . ." Jupiter began, but Pidgeon kept going.

Marge, the secretary, shrugged again. "You heard him, boys. I suggest you give me a call this afternoon."

As they left the bank Jupe said, "Mr. Pidgeon looked nervous to me."

"He sure did—after one glance at us." Bob frowned. "What did we ever do to him to get brushed off like that? We never even met the guy."

Pete shrugged. "I guess we'll find out this afternoon."

But when they returned later that day, Marge greeted them at her desk by shaking her head. "I'm sorry, boys, you really should have called. Mr. Pidgeon had to leave the bank early today—some sort of emergency."

"How unfortunate," Jupe said in his best adult voice. "This is a rather important matter. I don't suppose you could give us his home number?"

"You suppose right," Marge said. "That's against bank policy."

"Then perhaps we could arrange an appointment with him for tomorrow?"

"I'm afraid not." Marge didn't quite meet Jupe's eye as she said that. Before he could speak again, she hurried on. "In fact, he's pretty well booked up for the rest of the week."

Jupe's lips tightened. "I see," he said. "Well, perhaps we'll call you later in the week." He led the way out.

"What gives?" Pete asked.

"We were very politely and efficiently blown off," Jupe said bitterly. "They must think we're pretty dumb to swallow that 'called away' garbage."

"There's an easy way to check it out," Pete said. Instead of turning toward his car, he set off across the lot toward a section with a sign marked RESERVED PARKING—EXECUTIVES ONLY.

The area was filled with Mercedeses—but only one was forest-green. When the Investigators got close enough to read the plaque over the parking space, they weren't surprised to find Clayton Pidgeon's name on it.

"So it *is* a lie—unless he walked home," Bob said. "You know, if we're willing to wait him out, sooner or later he'll come get his car."

"I've got a better idea," Pete said, grinning. "Let's do it in style."

He led the way to the nearest pay phone, then uncrumpled the piece of paper Lynn Bolt had given him and punched in her number.

"Lynn? Hi, it's Pete Crenshaw . . . Yeah, it's good to talk to you too. Were you serious when you said you wanted to help us?" He smiled and nodded to the other Investigators. "Great! We need some stuff and you're the only person I know who can lend it to us."

He described what he needed, promised to be over to pick it up shortly, then turned to his baffled-looking friends. "Okay—first a stop at the nearest army-navy store, then we go to Lynn Bolt's house."

◆   ◆   ◆

They sat in the car as the end of banking hours came. Most of the cars cleared out of the lot. Then came the end of business hours, and the tellers and clerks left. There were still lots of cars in the executive area, however—including Clayton Pidgeon's Mercedes.

Ten minutes passed. "Suppose we're wrong about this?" Bob suddenly asked. "What if Pidgeon really did leave early in another car—and Vince Zappa just delivered this one late?"

"Executives don't leave on the dot of quitting time—especially new ones," Jupe said. "It looks bad."

About half an hour after the official closing time a guard opened the bank door, and out came Clayton Pidgeon. Wearing a blue pinstriped suit and carrying a briefcase, he hardly looked like the camouflaged, gun-toting commando leader of Saturday.

"All right, let's go." Pete now sat in the Firebird's front passenger seat, Bob was in back, and Jupe was behind the wheel. "And Jupe—don't burn out my transmission."

Jupe stomped hard on the accelerator, and the Firebird shot across the parking lot. He cut the wheel, and the car screeched into a tight turn, coming to rest with its broadside facing the rear of Pidgeon's Mercedes.

The bank officer's car couldn't move. A wall blocked it in front, and Pete's car cut it off in back. Pidgeon got out of his Mercedes, looking furious. "What kind of crazy stunt was that? I ought to—"

His voice cut off as Jupe stepped out of Pete's car and Pidgeon recognized him. Jupe saw a flash of alarm cross the man's face, then even more anger. "Look, kid, you've just made a big mistake."

Fists clenched, Pidgeon took a couple of steps in Jupe's direction. But Jupe merely shook his head and pointed to the two passenger windows, which faced the banker. Bob and Pete, dressed in brand-new camouflage shirts, leaned out, aiming two of Lynn Bolt's paint guns at him.

Pidgeon took a step back, his frantic eyes darting from the paint guns to the bank door. "Are you guys crazy?" he hissed. "There's a guard looking out the front window. If he sees those guns, he'll think this is a robbery—and in five seconds this lot will be crawling with cops!"

7

The War Store

"OH, WE HAVE NO INTENTION OF ROBBING ANYTHING,
Mr. Pidgeon, except perhaps a few minutes of
your time," Jupe said. "You *will* talk to us now?"

Clayton Pidgeon looked pleadingly at Jupe. "Yes!
Just put those stupid things away!"

Bob and Pete put down their paint guns, and Pidgeon breathed a sigh of relief. Then he turned to Jupe
and demanded, "What do you clowns want, anyway?
If you were hoping your clever commando attack
would impress me so much that I'd take you on as
recruits for Gorilla Warfare, I've got sad news for you.
The team's disbanding at the end of this month."

"Disbanding?" Pete said.

Pidgeon nodded. "Paintball has just become too
much. I'm a vice-president now, dealing with important clients. I can't afford to be known as a guy who
runs around shooting people on weekends—that kind
of embarrassment would hurt my career. So I'm taking
up golf instead."

"It might be a worse embarrassment for you if the bank got robbed," Jupe said.

Pidgeon stared at him for a long moment. "What are you talking about?"

"I'm talking about something that happened to my friend here Saturday while we were playing on Battleground Three," Jupe said. "Want to tell him, Pete?"

"In the first game all my friends got wiped out and I was hiding," Pete began the story. "These two guys came past me—they were talking about ripping off a safe with a cool million in it."

He paused as the banker's face went gray. "Does that mean something to you?" Jupe asked.

Pidgeon cleared his throat. "N-no. Go on with your story. Could you identify these two men?"

Pete shook his head. "I only saw their feet and ankles. One wore normal army camouflage. The other had that special gray-brown Rhodesian camouflage, like—"

"Like I had on," Pidgeon finished for him, getting even more upset. "But I wasn't the only one wearing that."

"There were four others," Jupe said. "Arthur Tillary, Vince Zappa, Splat Rodman, and another man from your team."

"Gunnar Olson," Pidgeon said. "He's second in command of Gorilla Warfare. An ex-Marine gunnery sergeant. Gunney, as we call him, trained us into a good fighting unit."

"And in spite of that, you're breaking up the team," Jupe said.

"That's not my doing," Pidgeon answered. "When I said I was going to leave, the other team members voted. They're businessmen, managers, most of them—and they don't like the way Gunney talks to them. He's like a drill sergeant ordering around a lot of dense recruits."

"So when you pulled out, they voted to disband rather than be commanded by him." Jupe frowned in thought. "You know, that gives Olson a fairly powerful motive to hold up your bank. He'd be revenged against you—through your bank—plus get his hands on a million dollars. That might be tempting."

"No—it's impossible," Pidgeon said. "I'd never believe Gunney would do such a thing." The look on his face, though, showed that Pidgeon did indeed believe it was at least possible.

"What does Olson do when he's not being second in command?" Pete asked.

"He's got a store in Burbank," Pidgeon said. "It's sort of a combined army surplus–survival–paintball shop."

Bob took down the address of Olson's store and the Investigators got ready to leave.

Pidgeon said to them, "Look, guys, I don't believe a word of this fairy tale." He gave them a nervous smile. "But if by chance you hear anything more about a robbery plan, let me know, okay? Don't leave me out of the loop."

"Right," Jupe said, getting into the front passenger seat of Pete's car. He watched Pidgeon hurriedly scramble into his Mercedes.

"Something's bugging that guy," Jupe said.

Pete started the Firebird and drove out of the lot. "Maybe he didn't want to get paint all over his new suit."

"Scared for his high-powered new job, maybe." Jupe shrugged. "He was definitely spooked when we mentioned a robbery, no matter what he says. Pete, first thing tomorrow, go check out Olson's store."

"Why am I the lucky one?" Pete complained.

" 'Cause you've got the build to blend in with his jock customers," Jupe said.

"Just another Rambo," Bob added.

"Hey, cut it out," Pete said.

The three guys drove off laughing.

◆   ◆   ◆

The next morning Pete parked his car on Burbank Avenue, just down the block from a store with a large sign reading GUNNEY'S SHACK and decorated with a Marine Corps insignia.

Walking inside, he found himself confronted with aisles and aisles of the most incredible stuff he'd ever seen. Uniforms from every American armed service—and those from about six other countries—fought for space with inflatable fishing rafts, crossbows, and laser-rifle sights.

Pete made his way down an aisle of mess kits, helmets, and six kinds of long wool underwear to a counter at the rear of the store. It seemed unattended. Then a man popped up from behind it—with a pistol in his hand.

Pete leaped back, then recognized the man as Gunnar Olson—and realized that the weapon in Olson's hand was a paint gun.

Olson looked as surprised as Pete felt. "Oh, sorry! I didn't think anybody was in the store."

He turned to a doorway behind the counter. "Can you give me a minute? I've got a customer in here."

Pete said, "Go on and take care of your business first. Hey, that's some gun you've got there."

"It's a special competition model. I just fitted it with this new scope." He looked at Pete. "Wait a second!" He slammed his hand on the counter. "I saw you playing at Battleground Three this weekend. You're the newbie who covered Lynn Bolt when she made that run with the flag."

Pete felt embarrassed. "Yeah—that was me."

Olson grinned. "Look, I've got a guy waiting for this on the target range out back. Give me a second, okay?"

He went out the doorway behind him. Then Pete heard the front door of the store open and turned to see Lynn Bolt smiling at him. "Hey, Pete!" she exclaimed. "What are you doing here? Need some more props?"

He smiled back. "Nah, the guns you lent us were just fine."

"I'm just sorry I wasn't around yesterday evening when you brought them back," she said. "I would have liked to see you again."

"Well, you're seeing me now," Pete said, feeling a little nervous. Somehow thinking about Lynn was easier than actually being with her. "What brings you here?"

Lynn stared. "Are you kidding? Gunney's place is like the local clubhouse for paintball fans. He sells us our supplies, fixes our guns, and if we're real lucky, gives us some advice. Lots of people hang out here." She came a little closer. "He's also got a firing range out back, but I'd rather you came and used mine."

"Uh, yeah." Kelly's angry face flashed into Pete's mind. He was really glad to see Olson return.

"Hey, Lynn," the red-haired man said. "I think we've got a new recruit here."

"I saw him first," Lynn told Olson.

Pete suddenly wished he were in Pittsburgh.

Olson laughed. "I thought the Ladykillers were all supposed to be girls."

Lynn shrugged. "We might let a few of the right kind of guys in."

"Got room for an old Gunney?" Olson asked. "The guys on Gorilla Warfare voted to break up rather than risk me being captain." He slammed his hand on the counter again. "Can you beat that?"

"But Gunney," Lynn said, "you *made* that team. Without you they were—"

"A bunch of corporate paper-pushers with soft guts," Olson growled. "I shaped them up like any sergeant shapes up a bunch of raw recruits."

He sneered. "But that's not the way you're *supposed* to talk to an assistant manager—much less a vice-president. That Pidgeon and his precious bank. Since he got promoted, he thinks he's a cut above us. And his pals—well, I made them into a fighting squad, so now they thank me by giving me the shaft."

"That's funny," Pete said with a laugh. "This is one sport where the training could come in handy. Like if you wanted to rob a bank or something . . ."

"What kind of lamebrained idea is that?" Olson barked. "That's the kind of dumb thing people have said about paintball for years. It's for Rambos, gun crazies, and maniacs. That's all garbage. It's a *game*, that's all. I *don't* train bank robbers, and you'd better get that straight." His voice was loud and angry.

"Okay, okay," Pete said. "Look, I've got to take care of a few errands. I'll catch you later." And maybe he would—after Olson cooled down. "Lynn, I'll see you around."

"Bet on it," she told him.

Pete got into his car and drove back to The Jones Salvage Yard. Once there, he headed for the old trailer The Three Investigators called Headquarters. It had one door opening on the junkyard and a few small, high windows. Inside he found Jupe, Bob, and Kelly sitting around Jupe's desk. Pete's eyes widened when he saw Kelly.

"Hi, Kelly," Pete said.

"Hi, yourself," she answered.

"What . . . ?"

"I've decided to help you guys solve this case," she announced. "And make sure what belongs to me doesn't do a bolt," she added.

Pete swallowed hard.

Fortunately Jupe's stomach rumbled at that moment. "Er, guys," he said, "it's about time for my midday meal . . ."

"Why can't you say 'lunch' like other people?" Bob complained.

Jupe ignored him. "So Pete, why don't you tell us what you found out at Olson's, and then we'll take a break."

"Right," Pete said, still standing, his back to the open door. "Olson is pretty mad at his paintball team, and at Pidgeon and his new bank title. But when I asked him about using paintball to train for a bank robbery, he nearly bit my head off."

Pete started pacing back and forth. "So if you ask me, I think—*agh!*" Pete jerked and fell to the floor.

Kelly screamed in horror as she looked at his back— and found a growing red stain!

8

The Silent Sniper

"HE'S DEAD!" KELLY MOANED. "OH, PETE, I TAKE BACK everything I said!" Then she gave a louder scream as Pete's dead body leaped up from the floor—very alive and very angry.

"Somebody just shot me with a paint gun," Pete yelled. "And they're going to be real sorry!"

He spun around and ran out the trailer door. "There he is—sneaking past that zebra!"

Titus Jones, Jupe's uncle, was famous for the quality—and the strangeness—of the things he salvaged. Where else could you find a menagerie of twenty-five animals rescued from dismantled carousels?

Pete only got a glimpse of a figure darting among the garish wooden animals. He raced in pursuit, the other Investigators and Kelly close behind him.

Pete was catching up as the intruder ran into the section reserved for architectural trimmings saved from old houses. At least, Pete was catching up until he found a heavy wooden trellis toppling toward him.

He ducked aside, but that let the attacker gain a considerable lead.

"The gate!" Pete yelled to his friends. "Guard the gate!"

Too late. They could hear the roar of a car engine, then the squeal of tires as a car took off. Pete sprinted for the junkyard gate. Just inside was Jupe's black Escort. "Jupe—your car keys!" Pete yelled.

Jupe dug them out and tossed them quickly. Pete caught them on the fly, one-handed, and jumped behind the wheel of the Ford. He revved the engine, then sent the car shooting out of the yard. A loud *pop* filled the air. But it wasn't the sound of a paint gun firing. It was the noise of a tire blowing out.

The car lurched, trying to hurl itself across the street toward the Jones house. Pete fought the wheel to straighten the car out. He almost succeeded—then another tire blew.

"My car!" Jupe wailed.

The Escort spun out of control. Clenching his teeth, Pete pumped the brakes. Then he saw the salvage yard fence coming straight at him.

Jupe wanted to cover his eyes, but he was mesmerized by the destruction underway.

The Escort plowed right through the wooden fence, its windshield shattering. Then it smacked into a marble column left out for display. The column tottered and its top section was dislodged. The top finally fell to flatten the Escort's roof. The rest of the marble mangled the car's hood.

Pete's friends rushed over. Miraculously, Pete was unhurt. They helped him get shakily out of the car.

"My baby," Kelly said, her face still pale from both of Pete's narrow escapes.

Jupe stood staring at his Escort. The Ford was a total loss. Besides the body damage it had sustained, the crazy angle of the front wheels showed that the axle had snapped.

"My car!" Jupe shouted. "How could you do this to me? I've been saving for months! I had it only three weeks and now it's totaled! Why me? Why is it always *my* car?"

"Have you lost your grip?" Bob demanded. "Pete could have been killed."

Jupe went red.

"Hey, guys, get a load of this." Kelly bent over and picked up something from the road. "That creep must have thrown this out to keep you from following."

She held up a foot-long piece of wood. It looked like plain round doweling, but three rows of nails had been hammered through it. No matter how the piece of wood fell, a row of nails would stick up—to do a number on the tires of any car that might pass by.

"These contraptions are called 'caltrops,'" Jupe said. "Look, there are more. Help me get them out of the way before they wreck somebody else's car."

They cleared the caltrops off the road, then rolled the Escort into the salvage yard. Next they got to work nailing plywood over the hole in the fence.

Jupe ground his teeth as he hammered. It was bad

enough being too heavy and not knowing how to flirt with girls, but being a teenager in Southern California without a car—that just tied it. Okay, get your mind back on the case, he told himself. That's what matters most.

"It's weird," Jupe said to Pete. "I didn't even hear the shot that got you."

Pete's head snapped up. "It was just like the first paintball game we played, where a silent sniper picked you all off. Didja notice?"

"Hey, that's right," Kelly said. "And there was no pop today, either."

"I'd worry a lot less about how it was done today and spend a little more time on who dunit," Bob said. "For once, we have a fairly straightforward case of *B* follows *A*. Pete went to Gunnar Olson's shop and talked to him. He mentioned bank robbery, and the next thing we know, he gets shot."

Jupe looked at his friend, frowning. "Good thinking, Bob. Let's head over to Olson's place and find out where he's been lately."

As soon as they laid Jupe's car to rest, the guys and Kelly got into Pete's Firebird and set off for Burbank. As a consolation prize, Pete let Jupe drive. Pete hoped that Lynn wouldn't drop into Olson's shop this time. Kelly was just getting back to normal.

Gunnar Olson greeted them genially as they came through the door. "Whoa! A whole troop of new customers." He smiled at Pete. "You not only came back, you brought reinforcements. What can I do for you?"

"You can answer some questions," Jupe said grimly. "My friend was in here talking to you before, and you got a little annoyed with him. Then when he came over to visit us, something came through the door at him." He motioned for Pete to turn around. "This!"

Olson stared at the still-damp mark of the paintball splat on Pete's shirt. Then Olson realized what Jupe was getting at, and his face turned bright red.

"Are you saying I came after him and did that?" Olson demanded. "If you are, you didn't hear what I told him before. Your pal was talking about using paintball to train for crime. That's just what got me sore. If I went after him with a paint gun, I'd be just as bad as the flakes that people say play this game."

Olson's eyes blazed. "That's not my style, mister. If he really got me annoyed, I might punch him in the mouth. But I wouldn't go sneaking around taking pot-shots at him."

"Then maybe you won't mind telling us where you were about half an hour ago," Bob said.

Olson snarled, "I was here."

"And do you have some way to prove that?"

"He does," came a voice from behind them.

Lynn Bolt stepped out from one of the aisles, a pile of sun helmets in her hands.

Uh-oh, Pete said to himself.

"I was picking out some equipment for my team," Lynn said. "Gunney was giving me a hand—he was here the whole time."

Pete couldn't help noticing that Kelly's face was tight. She glared at Lynn.

Bob threw up his hands. "Well, it was a good theory while it lasted."

"I have a question for you," Jupe said to Olson, who still looked pretty angry. "The paint gun that shot Pete didn't pop when it went off. In fact, it was completely silent. Who do you know with a gun like that?"

Olson's eyes narrowed as he took the news in. "You're saying this was done with a silenced gun? Well, I know only one guy around here who could tell you anything about that—Vince Zappa."

Lynn suddenly looked stricken. "And Vince was just in here!" She turned to Pete. "He came in right after you left, while Gunney was still complaining about that crack you made. Vince asked Gunney's advice about a special piece Vince is rigging for himself. Then he left right away. I bet he recognized you."

"What's it to you?" Kelly snapped.

Lynn gave her a startled look and then regained her cool. "Oh, I care a lot about Pete. I wouldn't want *any*thing to happen to him."

Jupe suddenly realized the two girls were fighting over Pete, who looked acutely embarrassed. For once Jupe was thankful he had no social life.

"Er, getting back to the case," Jupe said. "Zappa probably followed you to Headquarters, Pete. If he crouched down behind some of the junk nearby, he could have heard your whole report."

"And gotten pretty nervous," Bob finished. "But would he have gotten nervous enough to shoot Pete?"

"I see only one way to find out," Jupe said. "We'll have to pay another visit to Vince Zappa's garage."

Soon Jupe and Bob were pulling up at Zappa's place in Pete's car. The front of the garage was deserted. But when Jupe hit the horn a couple of times, Vince Zappa appeared from inside the building, wiping his hands on a rag.

"My friend was so impressed with what you did for my car, he's offering to trade his car for mine," Jupe said.

Bob choked, remembering the shape Jupe's car was in at the moment.

"This one looks great," Jupe went on, "but will it run all right? I thought you'd be able to tell me."

Zappa seemed to have no other customers. He opened the hood and set to work checking out the Firebird's engine. Jupe kept asking him questions, keeping his head under the hood as well.

Bob, meanwhile, backed up and headed into the building. He didn't have to waste time checking in the office—he knew exactly where he wanted to go.

In the rear of the building he found the door, just as Jupe had described it. This time, though, it was unlocked.

Bob leaned inside, peering around. The room was small, its walls spattered with various colors. One wall

was given over to a panel holding small hand tools.
Under it was a workbench. And on the workbench was
Vince's special project—a paint gun with an extra ex-
tension on its barrel.

To Bob's eyes it looked like a larger version of the
silencers he'd seen in movies.

"What are *you* doing here?" a voice behind him
snarled.

Bob turned to face an angry Vince Zappa. "And
don't tell me you were looking for the bathroom. That
line's been used already." The mechanic's lips were a
thin hard line under his thick black mustache.

Suddenly a heavy hand landed on Zappa's shoulder. It was Pete, who'd come over in Lynn's car, with
Kelly as a watchful chaperone. They'd parked on the
street as backup. After seeing Zappa push Jupe roughly
aside and head into the building, Pete had jumped out
of the car and run after him.

Zappa stared at the growing audience—which now
included Jupe, Kelly, and Lynn—and finally asked,
"What's going on?"

"Why don't you tell us?" Jupe said. "Pete, show
him your back."

Pete turned around and displayed his paintball
"wound" again.

"My friend here was shot with a paint gun over an
hour ago," Jupe said. "And he was shot by a gun that
was completely silent."

"What's that got to do with me?" Zappa backed into
the little workroom. He stopped as he realized what
Jupe was getting at.

"You think that I shot this guy?" Zappa said.

The Investigators and friends all blocked the doorway of the room now.

"So, somehow you found out that I've been working on a paint-gun silencer and blamed me for what happened to your friend." Zappa seemed thoughtful.

Then he looked squarely at his visitors. "But I know how to change your minds."

Before anyone could reach Zappa, he had snatched up the silenced paint gun and aimed it!

9

Spy Scam

ETE LEAPED FORWARD AS EVERYONE ELSE RECOILED. IT wasn't as if Zappa had a lethal weapon in his hand. But people had been injured—even blinded— by a good shot.

As Pete moved, Zappa fired the gun—at the paint-spattered wall. And although it was a low sound, no one in the room had any trouble hearing a *pop!* as the gun went off.

Zappa smiled sourly as he put the gun down. "Quieter, but not exactly what you'd call silent, is it?"

"No, and the gun that shot Pete *was* silent," Jupe had to admit. "We'd have heard that outside our door—or on the battlefield where the same guy apparently wiped us out."

"So the Silent Sniper nailed you guys too?" Zappa said. "He's been driving us crazy for months. Everybody who plays in this area gets stung by him at some time or another. That's why I've been working on a silencer of my own—to play a little catch-up ball in the technology department."

"And you have no idea who the sniper is?"

Zappa shrugged. "Everybody has suspicions. I've noticed that whenever my guys get hit, the Cactus Crawlers—Flint, Tillary, Gatling, and those guys— are on the other side. But I don't have any proof."

"Excuse me, Mr. Zappa." A heavy guy with thinning hair and a too-wide tie appeared at the door—an obvious salesman type. The man looked at the crowd in the room and said, "Good to see you have some customers."

Then he turned to Zappa, saying, "I left a copy of your parts order on your desk—along with as many free samples as I could spare."

As the man turned Bob said, "Excuse me a second. You were in the office just now?" Maybe he should have checked it out.

The man nodded. "Yeah, I've been working with Mr. Zappa for the last hour and a half."

The Investigators and their friends looked at one another. If Vince Zappa and this salesman had been together for that long, then Zappa had an alibi for the time of the shooting.

"Well, Mr. Zappa," Jupe said, "if we get a line on the sniper, we'll certainly let you know."

He turned to leave, but Zappa called after him. "There's still the business of my looking over your friend's car," the mechanic said, scribbling a bill onto a piece of paper.

Jupe looked at the figure, sighed, and dug deep into his pockets yet again.

Pete and Bob snickered.

While Zappa finished his business with the salesman, everyone else headed back to the salvage yard.

"Don't you have something better to do, like oiling your gun or something?" Kelly said as she got back into Lynn's car.

"I love a good chase," Lynn told her. "And all my equipment is in *fine* working condition."

"Well, we've got two suspects with alibis," Bob said, after the group had settled in Jupe's electronics workshop. "Who wants to check on Pidgeon?"

"*I'll* do it," Kelly volunteered, glaring at Lynn. She picked up the phone, dialed the Coastal Marine Bank, and asked for Clayton Pidgeon. Then she cooed into the phone, "This is Mr. Rockwell's office, calling for Mr. Pidgeon. Oh, I see. Has he been at lunch long? Ah. Uh-huh. Well, we'll try him again later."

She hung up, then turned to the others. "He's been gone since noon, on a long lunch with the bank president."

"Okay," Jupe said. "Let's run through what we've got. The guys on Battleground Three wearing Rhodesian camouflage were Splat Rodman, Art Tillary, Vince Zappa, Clayton Pidgeon, and Gunnar Olson. Zappa, Pidgeon, and Olson all have ironclad alibis. Which might be suspicious in itself."

"How's that again?" Pete said.

"The guy who popped you," Bob said, "could have been the partner of the guy in the Rhodesian cammies. Remember, one of the guys in the woods was wearing regular cammies."

"Oh, great," Pete said, "that leaves at least twenty other guys to check out."

"I didn't go for Flint's attitude on Sunday," Bob said. "There's something weird about that guy."

"Oh, get off it," Pete protested. "Flint's not going to rob a bank. He's a cop."

"I don't know how much longer he's going to be one," Lynn said. "Lots of people have been telling me rumors that he's leaving the force. Seems he's a real hard-nose with suspects—and with the other cops, too. So he's thinking of chucking the whole thing and starting his own security company."

"Even so," Jupe said, "he still strikes me as being too much of a straight arrow to go along with a robbery."

"I don't notice you saying anything like that about Tillary," Bob said.

"That crew-cut menace is a bully," Jupe said, frowning. "He proved that by the way he played with me on the field—and off. But," he said, shaking his head, "that doesn't make him a thief."

"But it does mean we should see if he's got an alibi for when Pete was shot." Bob reached for the phone book. "Anybody know where he works?"

"I've got his business card," Lynn said, digging into her bag. "He's my father's accountant."

"How convenient," Kelly said acidly.

From the very bottom of her purse, Lynn produced a crumpled card with a large red blotch on it.

"I can't believe that's the way he gives them out." Jupe smiled as Lynn handed the card to him.

"No, a paintball burst on it."

Kelly made a face. "You carry paintballs in your bag? Gross!"

"Better a paintball than a Barbie doll." Lynn rose to her feet, looking at her watch. "You guys can keep the card if you want. I've got to run."

"Me, too," Kelly said. "And I won't be around tomorrow, you guys—the cheerleading squad's going to Magic Mountain. Catch you in the evening." She made sure that Lynn saw her give Pete a juicy good-bye kiss.

Pete had to grin. Lips as weapons.

Lynn pulled out her car keys. "Is there somewhere I can drop you, Kelly?" she asked with phony sweetness.

Kelly smiled. "How nice, but I wouldn't *dream* of troubling you. I have my own car here."

Acting exquisitely polite to each other, the two girls left Headquarters.

"They're going to kill each other," Bob predicted.

Pete shook his head. "I think they'll kill me first."

Still holding the business card in his hand, Jupe was thinking about the case. "We still have to figure how to get into Tillary's office. I'm leaning toward the delivery-boy scam, but Tillary's seen me before." He turned to Bob. "Do you want to try it?"

A little while later the Three Investigators were outside Tillary's office in North Hollywood. They'd made one stop before arriving there, at a deli where Jupe had bought what he called "the props." Jupe now sat with them in the front seat, while Bob prepared for his role by pulling out his shirttail and messing up his hair.

"Okay, what we have here is a glazed donut and a coffee with milk," Jupe said, looking into the paper bag on his lap. Carefully he loosened the plastic top on the cardboard cup. He looked longingly at the snack for a moment, then handed the bag to Bob. "You know what to do."

Carrying the bag by the bottom, Bob walked into the small building, heading for the office of Tillary and Co. The receptionist looked up as he came in.

"Delivery for Mr. Tillary," Bob said. "Coffee with milk and a donut."

The woman behind the desk looked surprised. "Mr. Tillary doesn't usually have coffee this late in the day," she said.

Bob shrugged. "Hey, they got the call in the deli and sent me over here. That's all I know."

"Let me check." The receptionist walked over to another door in the office and opened it. "Mr. Tillary? Oh, he's not here."

Bob followed her into the office, carefully shifting his grip from the bottom to the top of the bag. "Well, I still need to be paid for this—whoops!"

The top came off the coffee. About half of it spilled on the bottom of the paper bag, which promptly tore, sending the cup—and the rest of the coffee—all over the floor.

"Wow, I'm sorry," Bob said.

"Hold on a minute," the woman said as she rushed past him. "I'll get some paper towels."

That gave Bob a few minutes alone in the office, and he made the most of them.

First he made a beeline for Tillary's desk calendar. It showed the accountant had had a lunch date. That probably cleared him of shooting Pete.

Quickly Bob looked around the rest of the office. He saw the usual business things—files, framed degrees, volumes of tax laws. In one corner, though, he found some stuff that had nothing to do with accounting. Hidden under some file folders were a pile of books with titles like *Security Today* and *Corporate Counterespionage*, several gun magazines, and the Army training manual on infiltration tactics.

A piece of paper was sticking out of the manual to mark a page. When Bob opened the book, he saw a heading: INFILTRATING DEFENDED COMPOUNDS.

Then he realized something was written on the bookmark. Bob opened the folded piece of paper to find a sketched map.

There wasn't much time left. He spread the map flat on Tillary's desk and pulled a box about the size of a Walkman out of his back pocket. Jupe had lent him his current pride and joy—a pocket photocopier. He'd repaired the gadget by scavenging parts from about five machines that had gone to the salvage yard as junk.

Bob just hoped the thing would work. He turned it on, pressed the glass end to the map, and ran it over the paper. With a faint hum and a flash of light, the machine recorded the image and unrolled a piece of paper with the copy.

Bob tore off the copy and hurriedly jammed it and the copier into his pocket. Then he replaced the map in the Army manual, and the book on the pile. He was just stepping back to the puddle on the floor when the receptionist reappeared with the paper towels.

"Young man," she said, "I met Mr. Tillary in the hallway, and he says he did *not* order any coffee."

"You mean the guys at the deli fouled up? Terrific." Bob took the towels from the woman. "What a mess. I'll clean it up." He mopped up the coffee, rescued the near-empty cup and soggy donut, and threw everything into a wastebasket. With more apologies, he got out of there—fast.

Bob came out of the building wiping his slightly sticky hands and grinning. He still didn't know if Tillary had a solid alibi for the time of the shooting. But the mission was definitely a success.

"Anything out of the ordinary?" Jupe asked as Bob got inside Pete's Firebird.

"I think so," Bob said, reaching for the copy in his pocket. "Take a look at this."

10

Kellyvision

T HE INVESTIGATORS SAT AROUND JUPE'S DESK IN HEAD-quarters, staring at the photocopy Bob had made in Tillary's office. It was of a very roughly sketched map.

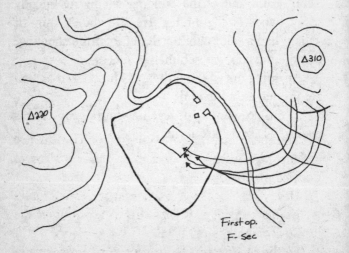

First op.
F- Sec

"That pair of squiggly lines could be a river or a

road," Bob said, pointing to the parallel lines that wound their way along the paper. "If it really makes that loop here," he added, pointing, "maybe we can match it on a map."

"Its shape suggests some kind of water, maybe a creek," Jupe said. He tapped the two triangles with numbers beside them. "That's a mapmaker's way of indicating the height of a hill. So we have two hills with a stream flowing between them."

"That leaves the big box, the three little squares, and the other line that circles around them," said Pete. He stared hard at the paper. "Somehow they seem familiar." Suddenly he looked up. "We've seen them before—they're set up just like those sheds and the sandbag fort at Battleground Three."

"Hmm," Jupe said. He turned the paper his way and studied it, pinching his lower lip. "The hills on Battleground Three weren't this high, and there was no creek. But the configuration of hills and sheds is exactly the same, like a smaller copy. But why . . . ?" He frowned at the map. Then his eyes lit up. "A practice drill for the real thing!"

"You mean that field at Battleground Three is just a setup for a robbery?" Pete said. "Like a place to practice maneuvers?"

"Hey, yeah," Bob said. "And those arrows are routes to the big rectangle. Routes that sweep *around* the huts—avoiding them."

"So the object must be to bypass the little squares and get inside the large rectangle," Jupe said. "I think we can assume the large rectangle represents a building." He read the note at the bottom of the map. "First op., F–Sec. What do you suppose that means?"

" 'Op' could mean operation—that has a kind of military feel to it," Pete said. "As for 'F–Sec'—maybe F-Section?"

"Or First Section," suggested Bob.

"First Section of what?" Jupe complained. "That's no help."

"Well, *excuse* me," said Bob.

"So we're back where we started," Jupe said. "We'll just have to hit topographical maps of the area until we find two hills, 220 and 310 feet tall, with a creek in between."

Bob didn't look happy. "And we've got only about 450 square miles of Greater Los Angeles to find them in."

They spent that evening and most of the next day poring over maps. Jupe had quickly ruled out most of downtown L.A. But the city had a lot of wilderness still at its doorstep. As soon as they started looking in the Santa Monica and San Gabriel mountains, they found hills, creeks, and canyons galore—all the way to San Bernardino.

"Suppose it's a *dry* streambed?" Jupe moaned as he examined a map with a magnifying glass.

"It's six thirty already. We've been at this for hours," Bob said, "and we've barely gotten past Topanga Canyon. At this rate the robbery could go down and the thieves be out of town before we find this place. We'll read about it in the papers."

Pete yawned, stretched, and rubbed eyes that felt like they'd been sandpapered. When someone knocked on the door to Headquarters, he leaped to his feet, eager to have something else to do besides go blind.

Kelly stood in the doorway, wearing a sundress that made Pete wish he'd gone along on the trip to Magic Mountain amusement park. "Are you a sight for sore eyes!" he exclaimed. "And I do mean sore eyes."

He led Kelly to the desk the other Investigators were working on. "Good news, guys. We've got another pair of eyes to search these dopey maps."

"Search maps?" Kelly said. "What are we supposed to be searching for?"

"Oh, right," Bob said, "let me fill you in." He explained about his search of Tillary's office and the strange map he'd found.

"Here's the photocopy I made," he finished, pointing to the sketch map on the table. "The prob is to match it up to someplace real on the city maps—which is driving us nuts."

"And blind," Pete put in.

Kelly was staring down at the little map, an odd expression on her face. "You're not gonna believe this, guys, but I think I know where this place is."

Jupe dropped the magnifying glass he was holding. "*What?*"

Looking pleased, Kelly went on. "Back in sixth grade, Mrs. Gastmeyer made us do this dumb map-making project, you know? Ellie Dalles and I drew a map of stars' houses in Beverly Hills. And this looks like Nils Forland's house. I remember drawing in the creek with that funny loop."

She grinned self-consciously. "It wasn't actually in Beverly Hills, but farther north. But he was sort of my favorite star, so I put his house in."

Pete stared at Kelly. "You really liked Nils Forland?" He remembered Forland as a very blond, handsome, and muscular actor from Scandinavia, who'd been popular some years back. The guy's accent was so thick that it sounded as if he'd learned his lines syllable by syllable.

"Oh, sure," Kelly said. "He had such blue eyes—"

"Before we get into that," Jupe interrupted, "maybe you can show us where this place is on the map."

"It's somewhere way up Benedict Canyon Drive, near—near Bella Drive?" Kelly's forehead wrinkled in thought as she tried to pull the street names from her memory. "I think that's it, but I wouldn't swear to it. I mean, it was eons ago."

Jupe was already riffling through maps, his magnifying glass at the ready. "Benedict Canyon Drive," he muttered, following it up the map. "Green Acres Drive, Del Resto, Beverly Estate—wait. Here's a Bella Drive, off Cielo." He looked over at Kelly. "It's certainly the way you described it—the area is just outside the Beverly Hills city limits. And there's lots of blank space around these roads—the houses must come with a lot of property."

"Well, that certainly saved us a lot of time—and

eyesight," Bob said, stretching. "Wonder who's the lucky dude living in that mansion now? Forland split to go home to Sweden, or wherever, years ago."

"Anyone up for a ride?" Jupe asked. "We can check to see if the place matches this map."

"And if it does?" Pete said.

Jupe shrugged. "I guess we find out who lives there and warn them that they may be robbed."

Evening was setting in as Pete drove his Firebird into Beverly Hills. Jupe directed him through a series of winding roads. They were halfway around one hill when Jupe suddenly looked up from his map and yelled, "Stop!"

Pete hit the brakes. If Jupe hadn't been wearing his seat belt, he would have rocketed through the windshield.

"Whoa!" Bob shouted from the back. Following Jupe's pointing finger, he quickly realized why they had just risked lobotomies to stop right there. From their viewpoint on the hillside, they were looking down into a small valley. A creek wound its way in a hook-shaped curve around another hill in the distance, then cut a fairly straight path along the canyon floor.

Beyond the stream rose the fence of a large estate. Behind it, several acres of gardens and carefully trimmed lawns spread out around an enormous mansion.

"Yes, that's the place," said Kelly.

They could also see the front gate—and the three

guardhouses that stood beyond it. Two faced the gate itself. The third was set at an angle along the curving driveway that led to the house.

"The guardhouses are set up exactly the way the shacks were at Battleground Three," Jupe confirmed.

"Bingo," Pete said. "Now we know where those guys are going to hit."

"But we still don't know *who* they're going to hit," Bob said.

"Maybe we can get some clues." Jupe tapped the pair of binoculars he'd brought along, opened the car door, and set off in the fading light. Shrugging, the other Investigators and Kelly followed.

Jupe led the way down the wooded hillside, across the stream, and up to the estate fence. "I don't have a whole lot of hope," he said, "but maybe we'll get lucky. All we need is a license plate, or *anything* we can trace . . ."

He leaned through the bars of the old-fashioned wrought-iron fence and focused the binoculars.

"That's weird," Jupe said. "There seems to be some kind of commotion near the guardhouses. Some guards are headed this way."

"Uh, Jupe," Pete said. "I think they're here."

The underbrush behind them rustled, then two grim-faced armed guards burst out to cover them. And the weapons in their hands were definitely *not* paint guns.

11

Fort Beverly Hills

"**H**OLD IT RIGHT THERE," THE LARGER OF THE TWO husky security men told them. "We'd hate to have to use these things." Both men held their machine pistols rock steady on the Investigators and Kelly.

For a second Jupe just stared, all words deserting him.

But by the time more gun-toting reinforcements arrived on the inner side of the fence, he'd decided on his story.

"What's the idea, spying on private property?" the head guard growled through the bars. He motioned with his pistol at Jupe's binoculars.

"Sir," Jupe said in his prissiest voice, "we represent the American chapter of the Nils Forland Fan Club. And how could we visit Los Angeles without seeing the site where Mr. Forland lived while filming such triumphs as *Red Eagle* and *Blutnoz the Barbarian*?"

Only in California could such a line have worked— but it did. Slowly the cocked machine pistols came down.

"Who the heck is Nils Forland?" Pete heard one of the guards ask.

"Guy was a muscle actor a few years back," came the answer. "He could never speak English. I'll never forget him in *Blutnoz*." The guard went into a heavily accented impersonation. "Eef yo dew nutt stond avay, I vill heff to kott yo en tew!"

The head guard was shaking his head. "Well, you saw your precious site. Now move along—and we don't want to see you back here."

"If we've offended the present owner, we're most sincerely sorry," Jupe said. "I'll apologize to him—or perhaps even better, write him a letter of apology. If you could please tell me his or her name. . . ."

"We're not paid to give away information. We're hired to keep people like you out of here." The head guard jerked his thumb. "Move it!"

The two guards outside the fence escorted the Investigators and Kelly back up the hill to their car.

"You kids are lucky you pulled this stunt when you did," the larger guard said. "After dark, they let guard dogs loose inside the fence. You go leaning through the bars and something might come along and bite your face off. The dogs are trained not to bark so intruders have no warning."

"Really?" said Jupe, fiddling with his binoculars. "I imagine we were lucky, then. We meant no harm. Please tell that to—whoever."

The guard just shrugged. "Frankly, I don't think he'd be much interested—he isn't a Nils Forland fan."

The guys and Kelly got into Pete's car and drove off.

Behind them, they saw the silhouettes of the two guards watching to make sure they went away.

"I think that officially shoots down Coastal Marine Bank as the site of the robbery," Bob said. "This is the joint the crooks will hit. You've got to say something for their nerve. I was sure those guards were going to shoot us."

"The place is really like a fortress," Jupe said.

"Fort Beverly Hills," Kelly joked.

"Whatever's in there sure has a lot of protection— just like those guys I overheard said." Pete frowned. "But we still don't know who's going to get ripped off."

"We do know he's a he," Jupe said. "That much was given away by the guards."

"And we know he's rich, to afford a place like this," Kelly added. "But how do we find out his name?"

Jupe smiled at Kelly as a devious plan came into his mind. "You're just who we need for this job," he said.

◆　　◆　　◆

First thing the next morning, Pete and Kelly staked out the road leading to the mystery estate's main gate. Pete sat in the back seat of his car, scanning the area with Jupe's binoculars. Kelly sat behind the wheel.

"Okay," Pete said, catching sight of a small white truck with red, white, and blue trim. It was headed down the main road. "He's coming."

Kelly started Pete's car and hit the gas. She intercepted the mailman just as he was about to turn down the drive that led to the estate. In the confusion, their bumpers smacked.

Pete shuddered, hidden behind the front seat. It was

all for the case. He could hear Kelly's voice. "Oh, I'm so sorry! Are you all right?"

Then he caught a male voice. "No damage done."

"But there's mail scattered all over your truck!" Kelly said. "Let me help pick it up."

After a few moments Kelly climbed back into the car, started it up, and took the road back up the hill. Once they had curved behind it she said, "You can get up now."

Pete popped up in the back seat. "Well? Did you get it?"

She grinned. "There was a whole bundle of mail about to be delivered down there. And the name on every letter was Samson Kladiti."

◆　　　◆　　　◆

"Kladiti?" Jupe said. "The millionaire?"

"That was the name on the mail," Kelly replied. "Samson Kladiti."

It was several hours later. Jupe had been munching low-cholesterol oat-bran muffins in Headquarters when Pete, Kelly, and Bob showed up.

"We met Bob at his dad's office," Pete said. "Mr. Andrews let us look at the newspaper's file on Kladiti."

Bob pulled out a page of notes. "The guy is known as the Gambler of Wall Street. He made his money by speculation, taking big chances on various companies. For instance, when Hooper Toys was nearly bankrupt, he bought into them heavily—and then they came out with those dolls, the Furry Family."

"I had one of them," Kelly said.

"So did every other nine-year-old at the time," Jupe

said. "So this Kladiti is famous for being brilliant—or lucky."

"Also for being rich and weird," Bob said, "though when you're rolling in it, they call it being eccentric. The story goes that he hasn't left that Benedict Canyon mansion for years, but he loves to gamble. So he's turned one room into a private casino and throws gambling parties when the mood grabs him."

"More and more interesting," Jupe said.

"Interesting, yes, but I've got a job to do." Bob headed for the door to Headquarters. "Sax is back from his week off. He asked me to put in a few hours and bring order to the filing system. So I'll be thinking mystery but reading about rock stars. Let me know what angle we're going to take on this Kladiti guy."

Jupe nodded, and Bob headed out the door to his VW bug.

Jupe reached for the phone book. "Let's see . . . Kinney . . . Klaber . . . oh, drat. He's not here. I bet he's unlisted." Jupe called Directory Assistance just to make sure.

"Yep, he's unlisted. We've got a problem. We can't call Kladiti to warn him, a letter would take too long, and those guards will never let us through the gate to tell him in person."

"Well, we'd better come up with something," Pete said. "I bet those guards took down my license plate number last night. If those paintballers do pull off a robbery, guess who the police are going to check out— yours truly. And I don't think they're going to buy your story about the Nils Forland Fan Club."

"I'll visit you in jail," Kelly promised him.

"Thanks a heap."

"But anyway," said Kelly, "do you think Kladiti would be dumb enough to keep a million dollars lying around his house?"

"He's supposed to be a kook, isn't he?" said Pete.

Jupe, who had been lost in thought, suddenly looked up. "I've heard that it takes only five people to get in touch with anyone in the world," he said. "All we need to do is find a friend who has a friend who has a friend who has a friend who knows Kladiti."

"Sure." Pete sighed. "Sounds real simple."

The only problem was, it didn't seem as if Samson Kladiti had any friends. Jupe spent an hour and a half on the phone trying to track down that unlisted number. He talked to friends, people the Investigators had helped on other cases—and friends of people they'd helped. He called in three big favors—and got absolutely nowhere.

Jupe hung up the phone and stared at it glumly. "So much for that theory."

Then the phone rang.

Jupe picked up the receiver to hear Bob's voice on the other end.

"What's the big idea of tying up the phone? I've been trying to get through for an hour." He sounded excited. "I'm at the office, and I just heard something that may explain what's going on at Kladiti's. Buddy Blue, the drummer for Scream, was just telling Sax that there's a big gambling party this Saturday at Sam the Man Kladiti's place. All the high rollers will be there—movie people, business types, rock stars. He even heard that Kladiti's having an armored truck full of money sent over from his bank . . ."

"Why do I feel you have something more to tell me?" Jupe said.

"Buddy said the bank was Coastal Marine," Bob finished.

Jupe's face lit up. "And I'd bet my pocket photocopier that the man who handles Kladiti's account is . . . Clayton Pidgeon!"

This time when Jupe and Pete went to the Coastal Marine Bank, they had no trouble getting in to see Pidgeon. But the vice-president wasn't happy to see them. He grew more agitated with every word they uttered.

"Unbelievable, unbelievable," Pidgeon said, mopping his brow with a handkerchief.

"I imagine this explains why you were so evasive with us the last time we spoke," Jupe said. "And why, even though you played down the possibility of the bank being robbed, you wanted to know anything more we found out about this robbery."

He gave Clayton Pidgeon a long stare. "Part of your new job includes dealing with Samson Kladiti. And somehow you let the news of his million-dollar withdrawal slip out."

Pidgeon nodded miserably. "Yes, I'm Kladiti's new personal banker. He called me three weeks ago to let me know about this withdrawal. The bank can't come up with that kind of cash at a moment's notice. We'll send it over tomorrow—Friday—morning since we're closed on Saturday." Pidgeon swiveled his chair nervously. "By accident I mentioned the kind of money I was handling when I told the guys on my paintball team I'd be leaving."

He looked over at the two Investigators. "So now you know why I was so shaken up when you came in here telling me about a million-dollar heist you heard being planned out at Battleground Three."

"And now we know the target." Jupe rose from his chair. "So perhaps we can leave the job of warning Mr. Kladiti to you—"

But Clayton Pidgeon shook his head in a definite no. "I'm not letting Kladiti hear a word of this," the bank officer said. "And I'm not going to bring in the police, either."

For a second Pete and Jupe stared at him. Then Pete found his voice. "What's the deal?" he demanded. "Are you afraid it'll make the bank—or you—look bad?"

"Look, guys," Pidgeon said, "I didn't get where I am today by losing my head and passing along every wild rumor I hear. If I warn Kladiti and nothing happens, the bank will look very foolish—and I have my career to think about."

"Of course, if the robbery does happen and you've warned no one, it will go a lot worse for the bank—and your job." Jupe leaned across the desk. "What does it take to convince you?"

"Proof," Pidgeon answered, sitting back in his chair.

"Give me proof that something is actually going to happen."

"But we just told you—" Pete began in frustration.

"You told me a lot of hearsay," Pidgeon said. "If I went to the bank president with that, he'd laugh me out of his office. And as for Kladiti—well, he thinks I'm the nervous type as it is, since I was so careful about arranging for that million in cash. If I go to him with worries about robbery, he might start wondering if I'm the right personal banker for him."

"So you're going to sit on your duff . . . and do *nothing*?" Pete couldn't believe what he was hearing.

"Watch yourself, young man," Pidgeon warned. "Kladiti is a gambler—he'd take his chances anyway. And I won't have him thinking I'm some sort of nervous Nellie."

"So you'll gamble too—with Kladiti's money," Jupe said.

A dull red flush made its way up Clayton Pidgeon's face. "I think we've all said enough. I've got work to do. If you find out anything else before the armored delivery tomorrow—anything *solid*—let me know."

"Oh, of course, Mr. Pidgeon." Jupe led the way to the door. "See you in the newspapers."

Jupe and Pete were silent as they left the office, marched across the banking floor, and headed for Pete's car.

"Jupe," Pete said miserably, "what are we going to *do*?"

"Keep on digging," Jupe replied. "I have to admit that Pidgeon is right. We don't have a shred of solid evidence about a robbery. It's all rumor and speculation. We don't even have a clue as to who's going to pull off this so-called robbery."

His face was grim as he looked back at the bank building. "I just hope we weren't in there talking to the mastermind behind the whole scam."

"Pidgeon?" Pete said.

Jupe nodded. "Because if we have, we've just warned him that his cover is blown."

12

Pay Dirt

FOUR O'CLOCK FOUND THE INVESTIGATORS BACK AT Headquarters, still trying to make some kind of sense out of their case. Kelly was out doing errands. Bob had finished his work for Sax and had returned to the salvage yard.

"Okay," Jupe said wearily, "let's go over it all again. We've got only one day left. Tomorrow night is the obvious time to rob Kladiti—when the money's there but not the party guests. Who are our suspects?"

"We're looking for a person who plays paintball, wears Rhodesian camouflage, and knows about Samson Kladiti's money." Pete reeled off the description by heart.

"That sounds exactly like Clayton Pidgeon," Jupe said.

"And Art Tillary, too," Bob pointed out.

Jupe frowned. "Tillary must be involved, but I have a hard time seeing him as the brains behind this. He's strictly a team player—a follower, not a leader."

Bob looked a little surprised. "I thought you'd jump

at the chance to nail the guy who gave you such a hard time when we were playing the game."

"Oh, I'm not forgetting how he splattered me at every chance—but I also remember the *way* he played," Jupe said. "Tillary is a grade A bully—but I didn't see any real traces of brains. Remember our game with the Cactus Crawlers on Sunday? Flint sent Tillary out to draw our fire. That's not the kind of thing you'd do with a valued member of your team."

Jupe went on. "Besides, if Tillary came up with the plan, why would he keep that map in his office? He'd either be able to keep the whole thing in his head, or he'd have a more elaborate map to brief the other people involved in the robbery."

"You've got something there," Bob said.

"And then there's the place you found the map." Jupe shook his head. "You said it was in a pile of gun magazines and manuals. That's escape reading for someone who's dabbling in adventure. But this robbery scheme is not a fantasy. It's very real." He frowned. "I just don't see Tillary running a show like that."

"Then there's Olson and Zappa," Pete said. "They both have strong motives. Zappa needs money, and Olson wants revenge on Pidgeon. But we don't have anything to tie them in to the Kladiti thing."

Bob suddenly sat up straight. "You know, guys, we're forgetting someone," he said. "A person who's into paintball, has Rhodesian cammies—and he actually built a practice ground for the robbery on his land."

"Splat Rodman!" Pete and Jupe said together.

"He'd have access to the best paintball players in the area," Bob said. "And years of experience in drawing up plans."

"Then let's find out how those sheds wound up on his playing field." Jupe got up and headed for the door. "Want to go and test Rodman's claim that he's open all week?"

The parking lot at Battleground III was virtually empty. But the Investigators did find a familiar face behind the counter at the command post. Lynn Bolt, wearing an orange referee's vest over a camouflage T-shirt and jeans, was cleaning a bunch of the field's rental paint guns.

"So it's the Three Investigators," she said, watching them come up. "Hot on the trail of another mystery?"

"I wouldn't say that so loud if I were you," Pete warned.

She turned to him. "Hi, stranger! Did Kelly let you off your leash?"

Pete was at a total loss for words.

"We were hoping to talk to Mr. Rodman," Jupe said. "Is he around?"

"Not right now. Splat's up north of the Valley, at Battleground One. He's paying me to lend a hand here to help get ready for the weekend crowds."

"Do you often wind up as a referee?" Pete asked, pointing at Lynn's vest.

Lynn shrugged. "Often enough. When the crowds were light and they were building the stuff on the special fields, they asked me to fill in a lot. It freed some of the hired hands for construction."

"So you were around here when the place was going up?" Jupe stepped forward. "Maybe you could tell us more about how the special fields got built."

Lynn shook her head. "You guys ask the weirdest questions. But fire away."

"Why did Rodman decide to build those extra things, like the shacks?" Pete asked.

"It's a way to make the game more fun," Lynn said. "More and more fields are doing it—some of the competition have setups that are really incredible. So when a lot of the team leaders started pressuring Splat to set up fields with a little more than rocks and trees, he listened."

"But it was the team captains who suggested the idea?" Jupe said.

Lynn nodded. "They even did some fund-raising, got hold of cheap plywood, and donated some labor."

"But who was the boss?" Bob wanted to know. "Did Rodman actually go out and supervise the construction?"

"No." Lynn shook her head. "Art Tillary designed the setups—and he supervised the construction himself."

"Tillary?" Jupe said in surprise.

"Art was a regular slave driver, measuring things out, hollering orders. He said he'd figured everything out scientifically, and he wanted it done exactly to his plans." Lynn laughed. "I've been in some of those 'scientifically designed' trench systems, and I think Art did a lousy job. There are some places that you just can't protect."

"Maybe Tillary had his mind on other things," Jupe said grimly.

"You guys are just getting weirder," Lynn said.

"Oh, don't pay any attention to Jupe," Pete told her. "*His* mind is on other things, too."

"Could we go over and check out one of the special fields?" Jupe asked abruptly.

"Sure—that's what most of the players are doing here," Lynn said. "We've got a small game going on the regular field, but a lot of the people just want to check us out—and get an idea of our terrain."

She looked a little apologetic. "You'll have to rent some safety goggles. Nobody gets onto the fields without them."

Jupe sighed and reached into his pocket yet again.

◆　　　◆　　　◆

The Investigators made their way along the bulldozed path they'd taken last Sunday with Splat Rodman and the Cactus Crawlers. It seemed a long time since they'd tried out those paintball machine guns on the training ground for crime.

"So Jupe," Bob said, "do you want to vote for chief suspect?"

"Not yet," Jupe grunted. "We've got two strikes against Tillary—the map of Kladiti's estate in his office and the fact that he seems to have reproduced it as a training field. But we also have to remember Pidgeon.

He knew about the money and when it would be at Kladiti's. And let's face it, he's also more the planning type. Plus he refused to alert the bank or the police about our suspicions."

They reached the Hamburger Hill turnoff and started off through the woods. Just as they reached the hilltop where the trees thinned, Pete suddenly grabbed his friends' arms, keeping them in the cover of the brush.

"There's somebody down there," he whispered.

A flicker of movement farther down the hill had alerted him. "If the guy had been wearing camouflage, I'd probably have missed him," Pete said.

"The problem is, none of us are wearing camouflage either," Bob said, looking at his friends. Jupe, as usual, was wearing a gaudy Hawaiian shirt—just the thing to stand out in a bunch of trees. Pete had on his red-and-yellow Rocky Beach High varsity jacket over a red T-shirt. So it was Bob, in a tan-and-blue striped polo shirt, who crept to the edge of the woods to see what was going on.

A few minutes later he came back. He was smeared with dirt where he'd gone belly-down to creep behind some bushes to get a good look.

"You won't believe this," Bob said quietly, trying to brush the dust off himself. "It's Tillary. He's out there sneaking around the sheds, timing himself with a stopwatch."

Jupe shook his head. "I keep telling you, that's not the way the leader of this kind of caper would act. He'd already have all the movements timed."

"Hey, why don't we just go down and ask him what he's doing," Pete suggested.

"Tillary would say he's practicing his infiltration tactics for the next game," Bob said.

"Right—he may be on the dumb side, but I don't see him telling us that he's practicing for a robbery." Jupe kicked the ground with his toe. "I don't know what we're going to do, but we'd better come up with an answer fast if we're going to crack this case."

Pete nodded. "Tomorrow the bad guys make their move."

13

Communications Problem

JUPE SPENT MOST OF THURSDAY EVENING ON THE TELE-phone, trying to get some kind of a line on Arthur Tillary and Clayton Pidgeon.

He talked to local merchants, a few bankers the Investigators had met in the course of other cases, even Chief Reynolds of the Rocky Beach Police. But the dirt he came up with wasn't even worth having the other Investigators dig into—as he reported to Pete and Bob on Friday morning.

"Tillary has a reputation for being a bit heavy with his hands," Jupe said, reading from his notes. "He tends to abuse people." He looked up and grinned at his friends. "You could find that out after spending about five minutes with him."

"Like you said, that doesn't prove he's a crook," Pete pointed out. "What else did you get on him?"

"People think he's a competent enough accountant, but no one thinks of him as clever." Jupe looked up from his notes again. "Lately he's been hinting about changing his business—talking to people about their security needs."

"That might tie in with some of the things I found in his office," Bob said. "He had books about corporate security in that pile of stuff."

"Corporate security and a plan of attack on Kladiti's estate," Jupe said. "It doesn't make any sense."

"How about Pidgeon?" Pete asked.

"Clayton Pidgeon is everyone's favorite banker." Jupe read over his notes. "He's zoomed right to the top. We already know he's the youngest veep at Coastal Marine. He works hard—"

"And he plays hard," Pete added. "The man said it himself—he spends his weekends running around and shooting people."

"I can see why he'd get off on zapping people," Bob said, "if he spends the rest of his week putting up with rich people's whims. What do your sources say about him personally?"

"People call him very ambitious and a bit of a stiff. His big interest in life is his career. And as far as everyone I've spoken to knows, that career is running just fine." Jupe ran a hand over his face. "The guy does not have a reason to rob the bank—or Samson Kladiti."

"Maybe we left out the obvious," Bob said.

"What's that?" Jupe asked.

"Because it's there? I mean, a million dollars *is* a million dollars. It would make a pretty good prize for a tough competitor."

"You may have something there," Jupe said. "It might even be true. But that's not something we can use to convince the police."

Jupe and Bob spent a few more hours on the phone. But they weren't even able to find a parking ticket in the pasts of their two suspects.

Finally Jupe slammed the phone down. "We're running out of time," he said. "We'll just have to warn Samson Kladiti directly. Although I haven't got a clue about how to do it—other than ramming something through his front gate and demanding to see him."

Jupe gave Pete an evil grin. "I don't suppose I could borrow your Firebird for that?"

"Why don't you just call him?" Bob asked.

Pete shook his head. "We tried that—the number is unlisted, and nobody we knew could get it."

"Well, *I've* got it." Bob went to the phone and dialed Sax Sendler's number. "Hi, Celeste," he said to his boss's secretary. "Could you do me a favor and give me the number that Buddy Blue left with us if we needed to contact him Saturday night? Right . . . Uh-huh . . . got it. Thanks." He scribbled on a piece of paper and handed it to Jupe.

"*What?*" Jupe cried. "You mean you knew it the whole time and didn't tell us?"

"Steady, Jupe," Pete said. "The clock is ticking."

"Sometimes, Andrews . . ." Jupe began as he dialed the long-sought number. The phone on the other end of the line rang. "Please, please," Jupe muttered.

Someone picked up the phone. "Kladiti," a deep, gravelly voice said.

"Mr. Samson Kladiti?" Jupe asked, hardly daring to believe his luck. He hadn't even gotten a secretary. He'd gotten the big man himself!

"Diss iss Kladiti," the voice said in heavily accented English. "Who iss diss?"

"Sir, you don't know me," Jupe began. "I'm calling to warn you that thieves will be breaking into your house tonight—"

"Anodder von!" the voice roared. Kladiti shouted the next few words so quickly, Jupe wasn't sure he understood them all. But he got the general idea.

Translated, Kladiti's tirade went something like: "So, you jokers think it's funny to keep calling me? I don't know where you got my number, but you can forget it. The telephone people are changing the number right now. Your story isn't even very original. I liked the one who called up to tell me a fighter-bomber would attack my house on Sunday morning. But you—phttt!"

"Wait! Wait!" Jupe begged. "The million doll—"

The phone on the other end slammed down, leaving Jupe's ears ringing and his heart hollow.

"The crook beat us again," Jupe said quietly, hanging up the phone. "He deluged Kladiti with a bunch of crank calls. Kladiti is so angry he won't even listen to me."

"Can't you call him back?" Bob suggested.

"No—he'll just hang up again."

"So what do we do now?" Pete said. "The cops will never buy our story but . . . hold on a minute."

"What?" Jupe said.

"Maybe we can't go to the police, but we can take what we know to a *policeman*—Nick Flint." Pete began to run with the idea. "I mean, look at it. Flint plays paintball. He knows the kind of skills that go into a winning game—the kind of skills paintball players build up. He's probably the only cop we know who'd understand the warning we're trying to give."

"Yeah," Bob said. "But will he appreciate it if we're pointing a finger at Art Tillary—one of his own teammates?"

Pete shrugged. "He may not like it, but we also know he's tough enough to check that sort of suspicion out. He may not be the nicest guy in the world, but he does seem like a real straight arrow. Besides, this is almost in his own backyard, workwise. He's a Beverly Hills cop."

"So what do you think we should do? Call him up?" Bob asked.

Jupe was already dialing the phone. "First we call the Beverly Hills Police and find out if Flint is on duty." He waited for a moment, until someone answered the phone. "I'm trying to contact Officer Nicholas Flint . . . yes, I see. I don't suppose you could—I thought that might be the policy. Well, thank you anyway."

He hung up. "Flint isn't on duty today, and won't be until Sunday. The desk sergeant didn't sound too unhappy about that. He also wouldn't give me Flint's home phone number. And," Jupe went on, riffling through the local phone book, "there's no Nicholas Flint in here." He looked unhappily at the phone.

"I'll bet Splat Rodman has Flint's number," Bob suggested.

Rodman did indeed have Flint's address and phone number, which he gladly gave to Jupe. But Jupe stopped as he went to dial the number.

"I think this job is going to need a personal touch," Jupe said. "And I'm not the guy for this one. Flint remembers me as the dimwit who tailed him back to the police station last Sunday. Pete, you shot him fair and square on Saturday. He might remember you as a crack paintballer. Besides, you can show him the only proof we've got—the welt on your back where you were shot on Tuesday.

"So I'll photocopy the map and make up some notes on who we think is involved. Suppose you run them over to Flint's house?"

"Suits me," Pete said, pulling on his red-and-yellow varsity jacket.

◆　　　◆　　　◆

Within half an hour Pete was driving his car through Nick Flint's neighborhood. The policeman had a small house on the edge of the Hollywood Hills. The neighborhood featured row after row of bungalows that had seen better days.

The road began to develop a definite uphill slant, and the area behind the houses became much wilder. Pete pulled his Firebird to a stop. The house with Flint's address was the last on the road, with a hilly rise behind it and canyons beyond. Pete figured the land was no good to build on, and that Flint was grateful for that. It gave him a huge backyard with no one to bother him.

Opening the car door, Pete got out. As he headed for Flint's house he heard a familiar sound in the distance—the dull *thwap!* of paintballs striking a hard surface.

Great! Pete thought. I caught Flint at home. He must be out back practicing his shooting.

But as Pete went closer to the house he realized something else. Sure, he was hearing the impact of the paint pellets. But he wasn't hearing the distinctive *pop!* of a paint gun being fired. Flint's gun was silent!

14

Dead Giveaway

PETE'S MIND WAS RACING. FLINT WAS THE SILENT sniper. He was the one guy they *couldn't* trust.

Pete didn't head for Nick Flint's front door. Instead he began circling the house, keeping brush between himself and the person practicing in the backyard.

His route took him up and around the shoulder of the hill behind the house. As soon as he was out of sight of the place, Pete ran up to the hill's crest. Then he lay on his stomach and slipped forward through the scrubby brush to keep from being silhouetted against the sky. His varsity jacket would get cruddy, but he'd worry about that later.

Pete inched his way ahead, careful not to rustle the dried grass and brush as he moved. He grinned. It was like using all the tricks he'd learned playing paintball in a final exam.

At last he found a nice patch of scrub that hid him but gave a complete view of the yard below.

Pete couldn't believe his eyes. Nick Flint stood about twenty feet from the rear of his garage, practicing his paintball marksmanship. But the weapon he was using for target practice was a six-foot blowgun.

Vince Zappa had been right to suspect the Cactus Crawlers. Pete had discovered their secret sniper weapon. The blowgun was completely silent—except for the noise when a paintball splatted.

In his yard, Flint quickly broke down the blowgun, unscrewing it into three two-foot sections. He slipped these under his bush jacket into some kind of harness. Obviously that was how the pipe was smuggled onto paintball fields.

Pete had to smile. In a sport where everybody bought high-tech equipment for a competitive edge, the secret weapon turned out to be something invented by South American Indians ages ago. Maybe the Three Investigators should have been glad that Flint stuck to paintballs, not poison darts.

Flint walked to the side of the garage, no trace of the hidden weapon showing. Was target practice over for the day? As Pete watched, he realized the answer was no. Flint unrolled a big sheet of paper and tacked it up to the back of the garage.

Pete squinted, trying to make out what was on the paper. Then he realized what it showed—silhouettes of dogs, big dogs. There was a side view, a front view, and a three-quarter-angle view. Pete watched as Flint again moved off about twenty feet. The man reassembled the blowpipe as efficiently as he'd taken it apart— obviously he was practicing that as well. Then he loaded and took aim.

A splat of paint marked the shoulder of the dog in

profile. Another shot followed, and full-face Rover took a splat in the chest. Pete watched as Flint continued to practice, leaving the silhouettes looking like large spotted animals.

Now it all began to come together. Flint was practicing his marksmanship on dogs—and attack dogs trained not to bark were released every night on the grounds of the Kladiti estate. This would be the perfect way to neutralize them and give a team of thieves free access to the mansion grounds.

Obviously, Flint didn't intend to use paintballs on the dogs. His blowgun must have come with some sort of darts, which he could smear with a little knockout juice. Pete didn't envy the dogs. He had been on the receiving end of that silent weapon, and it was no fun—even with a paintball.

So Pete had done more than discover the Cactus Crawlers' ace in the hole. He'd learned more about the tactics tonight's thieves would use—and he'd uncovered their leader. Jupe had been right after all. The careful planning for this operation was more than the bully Tillary could pull off. It had the fingerprints of methodical, military Nick Flint all over it.

Flint was probably one of the team captains who'd convinced Splat Rodman to build the special fields. Flint's teammate Arthur Tillary had designed them. And Pete himself had seen Flint training his men on the field. And what had they practiced? Sneaking unseen around the sheds in front of the sandbag fort—or was it avoiding the guardhouses at Samson Kladiti's estate? Pete wouldn't be surprised if all four members of the Cactus Crawlers were in on the theft—Flint, Tillary, Gatling, and Hare. Four arrows showing routes, four members of the team.

Pete lay very still, watching Flint practice. Okay, he knew how the thieves were going to do it and probably who they were. Now he had to get away to warn Jupe and the others without Flint spotting him.

Bugs began crawling over him, and a grass stalk tickled his nose. It was very bright in the sun, but Pete didn't even shield his eyes. He didn't want any movement to give his position away.

At last Flint disassembled the blowgun again, then took down the now-spattered dog silhouettes. He headed into the house, and Pete saw his chance. Crouched over, he got to his feet and headed for the crest of the hill.

Behind him, he heard the door bang open. Nick Flint came back into the yard. This time he was carrying his Police Positive pistol. "If you're going to go spying on people, kid, you should wear camouflage," Flint called.

He raised the gun—but Pete hurled himself over the brow of the hill. He ran down the slope on the other side, following a little trail that had been worn through the brush. He didn't know where the neighborhood shortcut led, but it went away from Nick Flint—and that was good enough for Pete.

Behind him, he heard footfalls and the noise of a body crashing through the dry brush. Flint was in hot pursuit. Pete's eyes darted around. He couldn't stay on this trail. It was opening into a straightaway, and that would just give Flint a clear shot at his back.

He veered off the trail, squeezing past a clump of bushes and making his way between a bunch of scruffy-looking trees. Crouched over to stay under the thickest branches, Pete ran along.

It seemed as if the whole hillside was out to get him. Tree roots twisted under his feet, trying to trip him. Branches whipped into his face. Scrawny bushes seemed to pop right out of the earth, determined to block his passage. And everything seemed to have unexpected thorns or stickers. Pete had a whole collection of twigs and small branches hanging from him as he ran.

And worst of all, his bushwhacking seemed to do him no good. Flint was still right on his tail. He didn't have to be much of a woodsman to tell where Pete had passed. The dry grass and brush crackled, rustled, and broke. The fresh damage was as good as a sign screaming PETE CRENSHAW WAS HERE!

Pete paused for a second to wipe the sweat from his eyes, his chest heaving. This final exam in paintball had suddenly turned very serious—especially since the other side was carrying a real gun. The only "weapon" Pete had was the tube of paintballs Lynn Bolt had slipped in his jacket pocket a couple of days ago.

With a million dollars at stake, Pete had no illusions about what the failing grade would be—death in an obscure canyon.

He set off again, angling to his right, hoping to lure Flint in a roundabout course that would lead back to Pete's car and escape.

But Flint didn't fall for the trick. Instead the cop ran straight through the brush, cutting Pete off. Pete's attempt to double back had only let his pursuer gain a couple of feet on him.

Blindly now, Pete just ran, zigzagging around trees, ducking through weak spots in clumps of brush. He didn't even plot a course but plowed ahead, keeping one arm up, elbow out, to protect his eyes from branches. Twice he tripped over roots, landing painfully on the ground in a belly flop. Once he put his foot down—and there was no ground there. Pete stumbled badly, just missing a sprained ankle.

That's all he needed, to be helpless and immobile in this miniature jungle, with Flint tracking him down with his trusty .38.

How had Flint known where to cut him off? Pete was yanked off balance when his arm caught on a very prickly bush. He jerked himself free—and watched the red fabric of his jacket sleeve tear. Then it hit him like a Mack truck. *The red fabric!* He'd been in such a panic, he'd forgotten to take off the telltale jacket. No wonder Flint had spotted him so easily. Pete tried to wriggle free of the jacket, but it was impossible while running at full speed. And there was no way he could slow down to get it off—not with Flint right on his tail.

Pete wasn't even sure which direction he was headed in now. He figured sooner or later he'd burst out into one of Flint's neighbors' backyards and make a straight run for it. Would Flint really shoot him with witnesses around? And with Pete's friends probably knowing where he was? Pete sincerely hoped not.

On the other hand, a million dollars was a million dollars. That kind of money might convince a man to take a chance. A big chance. After all, Flint was a cop. He could claim that Pete was a prowler, an intruder— a burglar.

These unhappy thoughts ran around in Pete's head as he crashed through yet another wall of brush—and found himself teetering over the lip of a canyon. He grabbed the trunk of one of the bushes, hauling himself back to safety—if he could call it safety with Flint breathing down his neck. The little cut in the ground was maybe twenty feet down and a little more than that across—too far to jump.

But when Pete went to retrace his steps, he heard Flint rushing up. No escape—unless he could fly. He looked down at the canyon floor again. Unless . . .

With a yell, Pete pushed back through the bushes on the canyon rim, making sure that Flint caught a glimpse of his red-and-yellow jacket. The cop came crashing closer.

Then, from fifteen feet away, Flint saw Pete fall over the canyon lip.

15

The Final Ambush

NICK FLINT STOOD AT THE EDGE OF THE CANYON, pistol in hand, staring down. Below him, he saw a body lying facedown. The legs were covered by brush, and the head was hidden by tall grass. But he could see the torso in that ridiculous jacket, and a small pool of red beside it.

That was good enough for him. Flint jammed his gun into his pocket and headed back the way he'd come.

Down on the canyon floor, crouched in a clump of brush, Pete Crenshaw breathed a silent sigh of relief. He was wearing the camouflage T-shirt he had bought at Battleground III. Clutched in his hand was the tree branch he'd used to break his fall. If Flint had come down to check the body, Pete had been ready to use the branch as a weapon and jump the man. But he'd gambled that Flint wouldn't want to come down. The cop couldn't risk leaving suspicious footprints or traces at what now might be considered the scene of an accident.

After reaching the canyon floor safely, Pete had torn off his jacket, arranged it to look like a fallen body, and mashed the tube of red paintballs to create the phony bloodstain.

The trick worked. Flint didn't come down to check things out. Pete gave him a few minutes, then carefully climbed out of the canyon. In the distance he heard Flint moving off through the underbrush. Waiting until he was sure Flint was gone, Pete started the slow business of creeping back to his car.

He was just sneaking out from behind one of the neighbors' houses when he saw Flint's beat-up Camaro pulling away down the street. Pete waited until the car had rounded a bend before he got behind his wheel.

The last time the Investigators had followed Flint, they'd been in Jupe's car. Even so, Pete stayed way back, more willing to lose Flint than to be seen and recognized. Luckily traffic was pretty heavy. All Pete had to do was lie low and see where Flint was heading.

He kept the man in sight all the way to the airport and up to the Aero Brazil ticket counter. After Flint bought a ticket, Pete gave him a few minutes to disappear into the crowd. Then he went up to the desk himself. "Excuse me," he said to the young ticket agent, "I thought I just saw a friend of my father's here."

"You mean Mr. Borden?" the young woman said, glancing down at the ticket stub.

"That's right, Borden," Pete told her. "My folks

wanted to throw a bon-voyage party for him, but he wouldn't tell anyone when he was leaving."

"You'll have to act fast." The young woman gave Pete a smile. "He's leaving for Rio tonight at midnight."

"I guess they *will* have to hurry," Pete said. "Thanks." He headed for the nearest pay phone, fumbling in his pockets for change, and dialed Headquarters. When Jupe answered, Pete said, "The case has just cracked."

◆   ◆   ◆

Pete and his friends sat around the desk in Headquarters trying to thrash out the new information he'd brought.

"He only bought one ticket?" Bob said. "That doesn't sound like a gang's getaway to me."

"You know," Jupe said, looking very uncomfortable, "a horribly reasonable explanation for all of this came to me while you were on the way back from the airport. Look at these elements—a cop who's rumored to be leaving the force and setting up his own security company. A friend of his who hints that he's giving up accountancy for a new career—and who's reading about corporate security. A single plane ticket to Rio. Suppose," Jupe said, "just *suppose* that we're not dealing with a robbery at all."

"What is it, then?" Bob wanted to know.

"A test," Jupe said. "A test to show the weaknesses of Kladiti's security system so he'd hire a new firm: F–Sec, Flint Security. After getting his new job, Flint takes a well-earned vacation."

Pete jumped to his feet. "Nice theory, Jupe. It only leaves out one fact." He leaned over the desk. "Flint chased me with a real *gun*. He left my 'dead body' where it was. That's not the way an innocent man acts. Is any vacation more important than getting help for an accident victim? And why is he heading off to Brazil under a phony name?"

"You're right," Jupe said. "But the only solid thing we could go to the police with is the ticket under the phony name. All the rest is still speculation and hearsay. We have no proof."

"We don't need any," Pete said, going over to the phone. "We know what's going down, who's doing it, and roughly when. All we need is some help to break it up." He looked at his friends. "Trust me, guys, I know what I'm doing."

Bob and Jupe both nodded. "Okay. It's your show." Jupe told him.

Pete dialed the number of Battleground III. "Hello, Mr. Rodman," he said when the phone was answered, "this is Pete Crenshaw. I want you to listen very carefully . . ."

◆   ◆   ◆

At nine P.M. Pete stood at the top of the hill overlooking Samson Kladiti's estate. He was dressed in a camouflage jumpsuit. So were all the people hunkered around him. In the near darkness he could make out Bob, Lynn, and Kelly, who kept giving Lynn annoyed looks.

"This may be the dumbest thing we've ever done," Bob whispered. Even so, his hands were clenched on the paintball machine gun. "And where's Jupe?" he asked.

"He's on the other side of the grounds," Pete told him, "in case they come out over there."

Kelly also clutched a paintball machine gun as she came over to whisper to Pete. "Why did you have to bring *her* in on this?" she hissed, glaring at Lynn.

"Why is everybody giving me grief tonight?" Pete wanted to know. "She's a great shot, she's helped us a lot during this case, and it's only fair for Lynn to be in on the payoff."

"*I'll* give her a payoff," Kelly began, but Pete cut her off.

"Shhhh!" he said. "I think it's beginning."

On the hillside below them four dark-clad figures slunk out of the trees and across the creek, taking a route calculated to avoid the sightlines from the guard-houses. As they came to the fence of the estate one man reached into his jacket, pulled out three lengths of tube, and assembled a blowgun. He slipped it through the bars of the fence and began shooting.

In moments all of the dogs must have been down, because the raiders scaled the fence and headed for the mansion. "So far it's going exactly as planned," Pete said. He raised his voice a little. "Okay, everybody, let's get into our positions."

They made their way quickly through the woods until they reached the tree line where the raiders had started. As they settled into their positions Lynn whispered, "How much longer?"

"Not much," Pete began.

Then his voice was cut off by a shrieking alarm in the mansion below. Lights went on, and the guardhouses began to look like anthills that someone had poked with a stick. Security people were running around, caught completely by surprise. Some headed for the house, others turned on flashlights and spread over the grounds. A searchlight on top of the third guardhouse sent a dazzling beam across the lawns.

Far from all the commotion, at the point where the raiders had gone in, three thieves were scrambling back over the fence.

This time, though, they were not coolly following some practiced plan. They stumbled and bumbled, their movements made clumsy by panic. Obviously they hadn't expected the alarm that pierced the air.

As the third figure vaulted to the ground outside the estate, Pete yelled, "Now!"

Then, with his friends and half of Splat Rodman's Splatforce III team, he stepped out of the woods to lay down a barrage of paintballs on the fleeing felons.

The tallest of the three—Tillary—instinctively reached to tear off his armband. His friends were yelling in pain and surprise as the paintballs just didn't stop. With wild rebel yells, some of the Splatforce paintballers went charging down the slope and over the creek, still firing as they ran. Guards were also converging on the area, drawn by the noise.

Surrounded, their commando suits soaked with repeated paint splatters, and faced with an arsenal of paintball and real weaponry, Tillary, Gatling, and Hare raised their hands.

Pete was already on the front lines explaining things to the guards. He'd managed his end of the counter-attack perfectly. There were no casualties—except one.

Lynn Bolt twisted around and looked at her back, which was crisscrossed with several lines of paintball splatters. "Somebody hit me from behind while we were charging down the hill!" she said. "I really got sprayed—by someone with a machine gun."

She gave Kelly a very hard look, but Pete's girlfriend was the picture of innocence. "Are you sure you didn't just wander into somebody's line of fire?" Kelly said. "It was so confusing up there, shooting away."

Sure, Pete told himself. He also reminded himself never to turn his back on Kelly when she was annoyed with him and had a weapon handy.

"We don't have them all," Bob said. "Where's Flint?"

As if on cue, they heard the popping of paintball fire from the distance—more heavy-duty volleys, with the rapid popcorn sound of paintball machine guns. And rising over all that noise came a howl of pure fury.

Security people escorted all of them to the guard-houses, where a few minutes later a grinning Jupe marched up with Nick Flint in tow, followed by Splat Rodman and the rest of Splatforce III. The master-mind of the aborted robbery didn't look too good. His camouflage suit was crusted with paint. One wild shot had caught him in the mouth, and his lip was swelling. The man's eyes were dazed, as if he still didn't realize what was happening to him.

"We found Flint's Camaro, which he stashed on the other side of the estate for his getaway." Jupe raised a paint-spattered duffel bag in his hands. "Then we just waited in ambush until he brought this right to us."

16

Double or Nothing

"GETAWAY? WHAT ARE YOU TALKING ABOUT?" TILLARY demanded. "Maybe we're trespassing, but we did it only as a test of the secur—"

Standing in the glare of the searchlight, Jupe opened the spattered duffel bag. The sight of the huge amount of money piled up inside cut Tillary's voice right off.

"Oh, I know that you and your friends just set out tonight on a little adventure," Jupe said. "You thought you were helping a friend start up a new business by testing a millionaire's security system and showing up its weaknesses."

The three members of the Cactus Crawlers nodded.

"You weren't. This was a robbery, plain and simple. Nick Flint was going to make off with the million dollars in the safe. And you and your teammates would be left holding the bag."

It took a few seconds for Jupe's words to sink in.

"There was no security company," Frank Hare said hollowly.

"No new careers," Herb Gatling chimed in. Jupe

realized he meant "No escape from my boring insurance job."

Tillary just stared at Flint. Then he said, "You set us up. You lousy—" He went for Flint, but two guards held him back.

"The plan was pretty simple—it was looking us in the face as soon as we saw the map. Oh, yes, Mr. Tillary," Jupe said, turning to his old antagonist. "We found the map in your office."

Flint gave his teammate a look that could have melted steel. "Couldn't keep it in your head, huh? You stupid—"

Now the guards had to restrain Flint.

"Three of the arrows on the map stopped at various points short of the box that represented the Kladiti mansion," Jupe said. "I suppose you all had some kind of job, or were supposed to watch and wait."

Hare nodded, beginning to get mad now himself. "I was the last one, posted outside the window to the den—that's where the safe is—to keep an eye on things. Nick went in to stick a cassette tape on the door to the safe—a kind of advertisement for Flint Security. Then we were supposed to call Kladiti from the first pay phone we hit after we left, so he'd get our message. Instead Nick goes in, and the next thing I hear is this kind of *whoooomp* sound and the alarm going off. I got out of there, and so did my friends."

"The noise you heard was probably the explosive Flint used to open the safe," Jupe said. "He may have known the location, but he didn't have the combination. That meant he had to blow the safe, which would also set off the alarm—and, as he planned, make his friends run in panic."

"But they wouldn't run very far," Pete said. "You parked your car on the other side of this hill, right, Tillary?" he asked, jerking a thumb over his shoulder. "Someone broke off a key in the ignition, so it wouldn't start—just the kind of thing you'd expect from a nervous amateur thief. I wonder who could have done it?"

Flint sagged a little in the guards' hands.

"But how did this guy know so much about our security arrangements?" one of the guards asked. Pete recognized him as the larger of the two men who'd escorted them to their car on Wednesday night.

"The guy who masterminded this robbery is a police officer," Jupe said. "He works for the Beverly Hills force. And though this mansion may not be inside the city limits, I'm sure the local police are interested in how the estate is guarded. Flint just had to read the file to find out about alarms, where the safe is, how many guards are stationed here, and where the guardhouses are set up.

"He probably thought he'd get some use out of his job, since he wouldn't be a policeman much longer."

"They were all angling to push me out," Flint suddenly snarled. "Bunch of weak-kneed bleeding hearts. They told me I was too rough on the prisoners. Then they said I was too rough on my partners. They were talking about departmental charges. Well, I'd show them."

"Before they could can you, you were going to

leave—with a little retirement fund, gotten with the help of three guys *you* trained," Pete said. "Of course, they'd have to take the rap. But the cops you'd worked with would know that you'd gotten away with a million dollars. And then you were all set to live happily ever after down in Rio."

Flint glared at Pete, suddenly realizing that the dead body he'd left had gotten up and followed him to the ticket counter. "It would all have worked—if you stupid kids hadn't butted in. How did you find out?"

"You told me." Pete enjoyed the look of shock on Flint's face. "It was when you and your pals wiped out my 'fresh meat' friends in our first game of paintball. I was hiding under a log, and you and, I guess, Tillary came by. He wore that Rhodesian camouflage, and you were the silent sniper in the tree-bark cammies. *You* were the one who mentioned the safe with a million in it."

Pete shook his head. "If I'd only been able to see your faces instead of your feet, this case would have been over long ago. Jupe immediately picked you out as the guy who'd plan an operation like this. But when we found out you were a cop, we got thrown off the track."

"However, we got back on track in time to foul up your little scheme," Jupe said. "There's only one thing that puzzles me. How did you know that Pete was investigating the possible robbery? You must have known, because you shot a paintball at him with the blowgun at our Headquarters."

"So you don't know everything, Jones," Flint said

in a nasty voice. He turned to Pete. "Remember when
you went to Gunney Olson's shop? He'd put a new
sight on a gun for a customer who was standing in the
target range out back."

"And that customer was you?" Pete said.

Flint nodded. "I was coming back in to ask a question about the sight when I overheard you asking Olson about robbing banks. That made me suspicious,
so I went out the back way and followed you. You
went to that trailer in the junkyard, and I heard what
you were saying inside. I thought a little shot in the
back would shake you up and get you off the case." He
shook his head. "Looks like I was wrong. But I did
wipe out Jones's car." Flint laughed nastily.

Jupiter gave him a black look.

In the distance now they heard the sirens of police
cars. While waiting for the cops to arrive, Pete was
surprised to see that Kelly and Lynn were chatting
together.

"No, really, Kelly," Lynn was saying. "You're a
terrific shot. I need women like you on my new team."

Kelly looked interested. Uh-oh, thought Pete.

Several L.A.P.D. black-and-whites pulled up, as
well as a carload of Flint's colleagues from the Beverly
Hills force. The officers quickly took the rogue cop
into custody.

The Investigators watched him go. "Well," Jupe
said, "I think that finishes this case."

"No," boomed a deep voice. From behind the
guards stepped a tall, heavily built man in a white suit.

Piercing dark eyes looked out at them from under thick white eyebrows. "Dat vass an interesting story."

"Mr. Kladiti?" Jupe said.

"I am Kladiti."

"We tried to warn you over the telephone—" Jupe began.

"And I hang up. I know." Kladiti shook his head as the police car with Flint in it drove off. "A real gambler, that man—he don't mind risks. Big risk, big reward. I like that."

At the word "reward," Jupe's ears perked up. "We took some risks to stop this," he said. "My friend here nearly got killed." He pointed to Pete.

"Nearly killed?" Kladiti's eyebrows went up in an arch of surprise. "*Very* big risk. So you should get very big reward." He walked over to the duffel bag, where the remaining police officers were counting Flint's loot. Kladiti waded in among them, plunged his hands into the cash, and came up with two fistfuls of hundred-dollar bills.

"Sir," a young policeman said, "you can't do that. This is evidence . . ."

"You mean you can't put dat man away if you count a few thousand short of a million? Don't tell me what to do with my money."

He turned to Pete. "I give you reward, or we make a gamble. You get this"—he held out one handful of money— "for reward. Or you get *this*"—he held out both hands—"if you win at double or nothing."

Jupe coughed nervously. "I think—"

"No, not you," Kladiti said. He nodded at Pete. "He took risk. He decides."

Pete made up his mind instantly. He'd been on a roll since that afternoon, when he'd discovered Flint was the brains behind the heist. "We'll gamble," he said. "Let's shoot the works."

"Okay!" Kladiti nodded his head. "What kind of gamble, now? You . . . boy," he said, whirling on Jupe. "You have a coin we can flip?"

Jupe pulled a quarter out of his pocket and prepared to toss it.

"Call it," Kladiti said to Pete.

"Heads," Pete said confidently as the coin flew up to twinkle in the beam of the searchlight.

It hit the ground—tails.

"Too bad," Kladiti said, tossing his money back into the duffel bag.

Jupe clenched his jaws in frustration. "You couldn't quit while you were ahead, could you?" he said to Pete. He turned to Splat Rodman. "Let me borrow one of those machine guns again!"

Another sizzling adventure!

THE 3 INVESTIGATORS
CRIMEBUSTERS # 5
An Ear for Danger
by Marc Brandel

Jupiter Jones has just won a free stay at a Mexican ranch, and he's hearing warning bells. The contest he entered was just too easy. Unable to resist the sound of mystery, Jupe accepts the prize—never dreaming what trouble will flare up in Mexico for himself and his sidekicks Pete and Bob.

For the beautiful ranch smolders with intrigue, and the Three Investigators get trapped in the middle of it. When a trail of treasure and treachery beckons them into the mountains, they don't dare say no. But can they talk their way out of danger before their dynamite vacation blows to bits?

A BORZOI SPRINTER PUBLISHED BY ALFRED A. KNOPF

Don't miss out on a single mystery!

THE 3 INVESTIGATORS
CRIMEBUSTERS # 6
Thriller Diller
by Megan Stine and H. William Stine

Suffocation II is going to be the next hit horror film, but the really spooky scenes are happening off-camera. The handsome leading man, Diller Rourke, has done an ugly disappearing act. The genius director is on a demented ego trip. And the big-bucks producer is weird with worry. Can this jinxed movie be saved?

Investigator Pete Crenshaw tries to do a solo job of scaring up the missing star, but the difficulties leave him gasping. He needs the smarts and the savvy of fellow detectives Jupiter Jones and Bob Andrews to dig to the bottom of the case. But can the trio unearth Diller before this thriller buries them alive?

A BORZOI SPRINTER PUBLISHED BY ALFRED A. KNOPF

You don't <u>dare</u> overlook...

THE 3 INVESTIGATORS
CRIMEBUSTERS #7
Reel Trouble
by G.H. Stone

Bob Andrews thinks he has his hands full helping a flaky band called the Hula Whoops rock-it to the top. But that's before he hits a sour note with a ruthless international gang who are busy pirating hot tapes with a cool disregard for the law. Now the pirates are after Bob.

Bob calls in his detective pals Jupe and Pete to help him dodge the rip-off artists—and keep those wild-and-weird Whoops from flipping out of the groove. The Three Investigators have got to crack this case and change everyone's tune...while bullets bang out the beat!

A BORZOI SPRINTER PUBLISHED BY ALFRED A. KNOPF